O 8/19

John Muir

Young Naturalist

Illustrated by Al Fiorentino

John Muir

Young Naturalist

by Montrew Dunham

ALADDIN PAPERBACKS

First Aladdin Paperbacks edition April 1998

Copyright © 1975 by the Bobbs-Merrill Company, Inc.

Aladdin Paperbacks
An imprint of Simon & Schuster
Children's Publishing Division
1230 Avenue of the Americas
New York, NY 10020

Printed in the United States of America

10 9 8 7 6 5 4 3 2 1

Library of Congress Cataloging-in-Publication Data
Dunham, Montrew.
John Muir : young naturalist / by Montrew Dunham;
illustrated by Al Fiorentino. —1st Aladdin Paperbacks ed.
p. cm.
Originally published: Indianapolis : Bobbs-Merrill, c1975,
in series: Childhood of famous Americans series.
Includes bibliographical references.
ISBN 978-0-689-81996-4
1. Muir, John, 1838-1914—Childhood and youth—Juvenile literature.
2. Naturalists—United States—Biography—Juvenile literature.
I. Fiorentino, Al. II. Title.
QH31.M9D8 1998
333.7'2'092—dc21
[B] 97-29092
CIP AC

TO

Denise and Jim—
my companions in search of John Muir's world

I would like to acknowledge my appreciation to Kathy Getz, who introduced me to the works of John Muir; to my husband, Bob—enthusiastic photographer of the beautiful places John Muir lived and loved; to Denise and Jim who shared with me the joy of discovery; to Helene Johnson who helped in our search for young John in Dunbar, Scotland; and to Dorothy Tinder, and Orilda and Paul for their assistance in California. I wish also to express my appreciation to John Jensen, Superintendent of the National Park Service at the John Muir home in Martinez, California; and Mrs. Plummer, granddaughter of John Swett; the Martinez, California Public Library; the Bancroft Library at the University of California in Berkeley; the Sterling Morton Library at the Morton Arboretum in Lisle, Illinois; and always my appreciation to the Downers Grove, Illinois, Public Library and the Inter-Library Loan Service.

Illustrations

Numerous Smaller Illustrations

Contents

John Muir

Young Naturalist

Seven-Year-Old Boy in Scotland

SEVEN-YEAR-OLD Johnnie Muir leaped from one round red rock to another. He crouched down to wait for his brother David, whom he often called Davey, to catch up with him. He looked out at the wild, rolling waves of the North Sea. "Johnnie, wait for me!" cried David.

"Come on, then," said Johnnie as he reached to help his younger brother over the tidal pool to the safety of the rock.

The wind blew shrill and loud through the rocks. Misty clouds rolled in the dark sky. David shivered in the chill of the bitter wind. He pulled his jacket collar up about his neck.

11

"Johnnie," he asked, "don't you think we should start home out of the cold?"

Johnnie didn't answer because he already had moved on. He had jumped across a tidal pool to see the crabs in the pool between the rocks.

John and David Muir lived with their father and mother and brothers and sisters in a big, three-story house in Dunbar, Scotland. Their father operated a feed store on the first floor and the family lived on the second floor above the store. John, whom everybody called Johnnie, had two older sisters, two younger brothers and twin baby sisters. Grandfather and Grandmother Gilrye, their mother's parents, lived across the street.

Father had told the children not to leave the back yard, but Johnnie and David just couldn't stay home. They loved to walk along the seashore and over the rocks and tide pools when the tide was out. They hunted shells and looked in the pools of water trapped between the rocks when the water was low. They watched the seaweed flowing back and forth in little streams of water. Sometimes they saw a wriggling eel or other interesting creatures.

Little wavelets rippled in the tidal pools, and the air tingled with a coming storm. Suddenly a flash of lightning streaked across the sky. "Look at the castle!" cried Johnnie. He pointed to the dark ruins of Dunbar Castle, which loomed up against the stormy sky.

David held tightly to a rock as he turned his head to look. "An awful storm is coming up, Johnnie," he said.

"There surely is," replied Johnnie. "Let's go hide in the castle."

The rough, rocky ruins of the empty castle clung to the cliff. The dark, cellar dungeons lay open on the beach at low tide. Johnnie ran to the first opening into the dark dungeon with David trying hard to keep up with him. A voice wailed down the tower of the castle. "Hey, Johnnie, down there! I dare you to climb up the tower!"

Johnnie leaned back and squinted his eyes to see who was calling. He could barely make out a shadowy figure against the gray sky. "Hey, Robert, is that you?" he asked.

"I dare you to climb that wall," his friend Robert repeated. "I'll bet you can't."

Johnnie looked at the wall with its sharp, jutting rocks. "Yes, I can!" he retorted.

David had scrambled up the cliff by the castle. From here he overheard the dares. "Johnnie, let's go home," he called.

"Not yet, Davey," shouted Johnnie. "I must try to climb this wall first."

Johnnie walked slowly through the dark cellars of the castle until he came to the high wall.

14

He felt with his foot carefully until he could find a safe foothold. Then he scrambled up with his hands to find a rock to clutch. Slowly and carefully he lifted himself up the rocky wall. Below him the waves lashed in through holes in the dungeon and filled the pit with foaming sea water.

Johnnie climbed on. His arms ached and his feet slipped on the uneven rocks. He could feel scratches on his face, and his hands were raw from clutching the stone wall. He could hear the waves below him rolling in and then pushing back out to sea. He knew he could not stop and he dare not fall.

It seemed that he would never reach the top, but finally Robert reached down to help him. Then he crawled out and sprawled on the floor of the turret.

The storm had worsened as Johnnie was climbing. Lightning flashed, thunder crackled, and the waves dashed higher and higher, pounding on the castle and the cliffs. David shouted, "Johnnie, come on or we'll get a thrashing when we get home."

Johnnie nodded. He knew David was right. He climbed over the top and leaped to the cliff where David was waiting for him. They ran across the fields as fast as they could to get home. Quietly they tried to sneak in the back door and up the stairs without being seen. "John!" Father's voice bellowed. "Why are you late for tea?"

Both boys stood still and looked down at their wet boots and dripping clothes. Father came up to them and grabbed them by the shoulders. "Get yourselves upstairs and change into dry clothes," he said.

All that evening the storm wailed and lashed. Sheets of rain pelted against the house. The cold wind whistled around the windows. Johnnie sat still in his chair at the supper table listening to the noise of the storm. "This is a pitiful night for the poor sailors at sea," said Father.

Mother nodded and sighed. "It must be a dreadful thing to be in a boat at the mercy of a storm at sea," she said.

After supper Father held the family worship and prayed for the poor lads in the lap of the storm. Then all the children ran up to bed. The boys' room flashed with lightning, followed by claps of thunder.

Johnnie wished he could slip outside into the storm. He closed his eyes and could imagine the angry waves clawing and pulling at the shore. Finally he fell sound asleep.

When Johnnie woke up the next morning the outdoors was clear and calm. "Johnnie! Johnnie! Get up!" called his sister, Sarah. "There was a shipwreck last night."

Johnnie ran down to breakfast and heard his father and mother talking about the shipwreck. "The ship was driven onto the rocks by the storm," said Father. "Thank God, all the crewmen were saved."

"How did they get ashore in such rough water?" asked Mother anxiously.

"The lighthouse keeper and his son rowed a rescue boat to the helpless battered ship," replied Father.

"Where are the seamen now?" asked Mother. "Do they need a place to stay?"

"As far as I know they are all at the lighthouse, drying out," answered Mr. Muir.

Johnnie and David could scarcely finish their porridge, they were so eager to see the shipwreck. They hurried through the garden gate and started to run as fast as they could. Along the way they met some of their friends. "Did you know that there's a ship wrecked on the rocks?" asked Willie excitedly.

"Yes," Johnnie said. "Have you see it yet?"

"No," replied Willie as he kept running.

At the same time another boy, Bruce, came running up to join them. "There's a rumor that all the sailors on the ship have been drowned," he said in an excited tone of voice.

19

"That's not true," retorted Johnnie. "My father says that all the sailors from the ship have been saved."

When the boys reached the shore, they saw the battered ship hanging on a red rock with its side ripped open. The rushing waves washed crates and barrels of apples from the ship. Loose red apples bobbed along on the waves washing in to shore.

The boys ran into the gently rolling waves to get some of the red apples, which were floating about on the salty foam. Moments later they sat on the rocks and had fun eating them, even though they tasted salty and tart.

War Games
after School

LIFE WAS ALWAYS an adventure for Johnnie Muir. He learned many of his first lessons from his Grandfather Gilrye. For instance, his grandfather taught him how to tell time on the clock at the top of the town hall tower.

Usually after school Johnnie and David ran across the street to their grandparents' house to study their lessons for the next day. Grandmother always had cookies for the boys, and the warm fire burned cheerily on the hearth. "Grandfather, did Cromwell really fight a battle at Dunbar?" asked Johnnie.

Grandfather shook his head as he told the

stories of the battles that had taken place at Dunbar. "Two of the most important battlegrounds of all time are located here on these red cliffs of the North Sea," he said.

Johnnie sat and dreamed of the courage and bravery of old Scottish heroes. He loved to hear the battle stories of William Wallace and Robert the Bruce. Suddenly he turned to his grandfather and asked, "Who once lived in Dunbar Castle? Tell me something about them and their lives, if you can."

"It would take a book to tell all that went on in that old castle," replied Grandfather. "King Edward fled to the castle after his defeat at Bannockburn by Robert Bruce."

"Was that when Robert Bruce won Scottish independence?" asked Johnnie eagerly.

"That's right, laddie," Grandfather replied, "but that wasn't the end of the fighting. Dunbar Castle has seen soldiers and kings matching

22

swords up and down its stairs and turrets, across its lofty precipices, and even through its dungeons."

Grandfather told Johnnie about Mary, Queen of Scots, coming to Dunbar Castle. Also he told about Cromwell, much later, defeating the Royal troops on the battlefield at the outskirts of Dunbar.

Johnnie's imagination soared as he listened to these battle stories. The minds of all Scottish boys were filled with the glorious tales of their war heroes. They had no doubt that sometime later they would all become soldiers themselves. Then they would win battles just as the other Scottish heroes had done in the history stories they read in school.

At Davel Brae School the boys often divided into two armies and played war. One afternoon after school Robert cried, "Let's play a war game. I'll be leader of one army." He motioned to the boys on his side of the playground to come and join him.

Willie answered, "Johnnie, you be the leader of our army."

Johnnie ran forward and called to his teammates to form an army behind him. They ran back to fill their caps with sand and pieces of sod. Then they formed a line facing the glaring faces of Robert's army.

Johnnie waited for a moment to make sure that all of his boys were ready. Suddenly with his hand high in the air, he charged forward, shouting, "Bannockburn! Bannockburn!"

The rest of the boys ran up from behind him, shouting and screaming, "Bannockburn! Scotland forever!" Then they swung their caps fiercely, hurling the sand and the sod at Robert's advancing army.

At the same time the boys in Robert's army pushed forward, throwing ammunition from

24

their caps. They, too, cheered and shouted, "Scotland forever!"

When the warriors ran out of ammunition, they fell back. Hastily they dropped to the ground and grabbed up more handfuls of sand and sod. Then once again they charged, and again and again they pressed forward until they finally wore themselves out.

Johnnie sank down on the ground to rest. In the distance he caught sight of a ship far out on the rolling sea. As it came nearer he noticed that there was another ship close behind it. "See the ships lining up to enter the Firth of Forth," he said.

The tide was coming in and the waves rolled higher and higher up the sandy shore. They rolled up almost as if they were playing tag. The dark green sea water, covered with white frothy foam, rolled almost up to the school wall and then went rushing back. Another wave came rolling in as if trying to splash against the wall. Johnnie could even feel the misty spray on his face.

"Come on, Johnnie," called Robert, waving his hand. "Let's go home."

The boys ran rapidly down the hill from school. Johnnie reached the bottom of the hill first with Willie, Robert, and David just behind. As they leaned against the stone fence, laughing and trying to catch their breath, Sarah came running up the road. "Come home quickly!" she cried excitedly. "The Scottish Grays have come."

"The Scottish Grays!" exclaimed Johnnie. He knew that the Scottish Grays were a famous troop of soldiers.

"They have put four of their horses in our stable for the night!" Sarah added.

Johnnie and David ran home after their sister. When they reached the back gate, they

saw the big horses in the stable. "How long will they be here?" asked Johnnie.

"Only until morning," Sarah answered.

The next morning Johnnie and David could hardly eat their breakfast, they were so anxious to get out to the stable. When they arrived, they were glad to find the horses still there. Johnnie took the pitchfork and tossed some hay into the feed boxes for the horses to eat. David went to the pump and brought fresh cold water for the horses to drink.

Suddenly there was a confusing sound of clatter back of the stable. Johnnie ran to the door to peek out. "Here come the soldiers!" he cried. "See their fine uniforms."

The soldiers sat down to polish their shining helmets and swords. They sat on the ground and talked and laughed as they worked. Soon one of them saw a nest of robin redbreasts in an elm tree. He climbed to his feet and managed to see three or four birds in the nest, just ready to fly.

Johnnie smiled when he saw how interested the trooper was in these young birds. He had watched the mother robin sit on this nest and hatch out the eggs.

When the soldiers got ready to go, Johnnie and David were proud to help them saddle their horses. "Just a moment," said the soldier who had looked up at the birds' nest.

He jumped down from his horse and went back to the elm tree. Deftly he climbed the tree until he reached the nest. Then he snatched the baby birds one by one and shoved them into his jacket.

Moments later the soldier swung astride his horse and rode away with the baby songbirds stuffed in his jacket. Sadly Johnnie returned to the stable, wondering how anybody could be so cruel to innocent creatures.

Daring Games about the House

IN THE SUMMERTIME Johnnie and his friends roamed the moors or countryside near their homes. They held foot races to see who could run fastest. They wrestled and jumped over walls. They climbed trees and hunted birds' nests in the fields.

One day Johnnie lay in a meadow for hours to watch larks soaring above him. Suddenly out of a nest hidden in tall grass a male lark flew almost straight up. Then, as if he were treading the air with his wing beats, he stopped and sang a beautiful, sweet song. Soon he flew higher and stopped to sing another clear,

30

sweet song. He kept going higher and higher until finally he was so high that he could not be seen at all.

Soon after the first lark disappeared, another lark darted into the sky and started to sing a song. Again the lark flew higher and higher until he passed out of sight. As Johnnie lay on the ground watching, he wondered where all the larks went in the sky.

In Scotland, during summer, when the days were long, children had to go to bed before sunset. One evening after supper, Johnnie and David slipped out of the kitchen to sit on the garden steps. Soon Mary Ann, the servant girl, came out of the kitchen and said, "You're supposed to be in bed. What are you doing here? Are you afraid of the doctor ghost next to your bedroom?"

David's eyes widened as he asked, "What ghost do you mean, Mary Ann?"

"Once a doctor used to own this house," Mary Ann started to explain.

Johnnie interrupted. "Yes, all his laboratory test tubes and other things are in the room next to our bedroom," he said.

"That's what I mean," said Mary Ann, "and all his skeletons, ghosts, and magic potions are there looking after them."

David looked at Mary Ann and asked in a fearful tone of voice, "Are there really any ghosts in that room?"

Before Mary Ann could answer Mother's voice called from the upstairs window, "Johnnie and David, where are you?"

Johnnie and David quickly ran upstairs to their bedroom, where Mother was waiting for them. "Hurry on into bed," she said. "It's already past your bedtime."

The two boys peeled off their dirty clothes and put on their long, white nightshirts.

Promptly they hopped into bed and Mother tucked the covers carefully around them. Finally she reached up and drew the curtains to shut out the light.

For a while Johnnie lay thinking about the big dark room next to them. He didn't really believe there were any ghosts in the room. The moment he heard his mother's last footstep, he jumped out of bed. "What are you doing?" asked David, sitting up straight.

Johnnie didn't answer but beckoned to David. "Come on, let's go into the doctor's room," he said quietly.

David gasped. "Do you really think we should?" he asked.

Johnnie opened the door slightly and peeked stealthily through the crack. Then he opened the door wider and looked in at stacks of dusty flasks, test tubes, and glass tubing. "Oh, look at all these things!" he said. "The doctor must have used them every night to make his medicines and tonics."

"What things?" asked David. His voice was shaky and low.

Johnnie walked stealthily into the dark room. He looked around at the dark shadows and hurried back out. "David, I'll bet you can't go in as far as I did without getting caught," he dared.

"Without getting caught by what?" David asked nervously.

"By the ghost doctor," replied Johnnie.

At first David hesitated because he was too afraid to go into the doctor's room. "Come on, David, and accept this scootcher," Johnnie urged. "Come on."

David swallowed. He was too scared to accept the scootcher, but he didn't want to refuse. "I'll do it," he said quickly.

He opened the door slowly. The room was so

34

dark because of the drawn blinds that he couldn't see anything. Before losing his nerve he ran in and back out as quickly as he could. "I did it, Johnnie!" he cried. "I did the scootcher!"

By now Johnnie was sure there were no ghosts in the doctor's laboratory. He ran over and opened a dormer window which overlooked the slate roof of the house. He crawled out the window and hung on the steep roof. As he did so the wind caught his nightgown and blew it out like a balloon. "I dare you to do this," he called to David inside the room.

David ran to the window to watch Johnnie. "Sure, I can do that scootcher," he said.

Johnnie climbed back inside and watched as David let himself out onto the roof and hung from the windowsill. Then David climbed back inside and Johnnie went out on the roof again. Once more he hung from the windowsill, but with only one hand. "What about doing this scootcher, Davey?" he cried.

"All right, I can do that, too," said David bravely. Quickly he climbed out the window and hung on the roof by one hand.

Again Johnnie crawled out and hung on the roof by only one finger. Then David crawled out and did the same thing.

Now Johnnie tried to think of another good scootcher. He stood on the windowsill and said, "Next I'm going to climb out the window and sit on top of the dormer roof. If I can't get back in, ask Father to bring a ladder to get me down."

Johnnie began to climb and soon sat astride the dormer roof. From this high perch he could see across the garden walls all over town. He held on tightly lest a howling wind blow him off his high perch.

After a few moments, he decided to try to

get down. He looked down at the garden far below and his heart pounded. Carefully he felt for a niche for his feet and grabbed a slate to let himself down. Suddenly his foot slipped, but he managed to grab another slate and low-

ered himself to the window sill. Then he swung his body into the room and sank to the floor, trying to catch his breath.

David started to climb out the window, but Johnnie grabbed him by his leg. "Are you sure you want to do this scootcher?" he asked. "It's really hard."

David nodded bravely and started to climb out the window. "Yes, I'm sure," he replied.

"You don't have to," said Johnnie.

"I know," said David weakly as he climbed on out. He climbed cautiously and slowly and managed to get on top of the dormer roof. Johnnie leaned out the window as far as he could to see him sitting high above with his nightshirt blowing in the wind.

"That's enough, Davey," Johnnie called. "You've done the scootcher. Come down now, but be careful."

David held tightly to the dormer roof and

tried to get a foothold to climb down, first with one foot and then with the other, but failed. All the while he clutched the ridge pole of the roof with his hands. Finally he gave up and straddled the roof again and began to cry. "Johnnie, I cannot get down," he sobbed.

Johnnie shouted, "Don't cry, Davey, lest Father hear you and punish us. I'll help you to get down."

Johnnie stood on the windowsill and tried to reach his brother. "Davey, put your feet down," he called.

David held tightly to the roof and slid his feet down as far as he could. Johnnie grabbed them and held on tightly. Slowly David slid down, clutching at pieces of slate as best he could. Finally Johnnie grabbed his feet firmly and pulled him in through the window.

By now both boys were so frightened that they gladly stopped playing scootchers for the night. They crawled into bed, pulled the covers up over themselves, and in a few moments went soundly to sleep.

Day after day Johnnie and David played and had jolly times together. They roamed through meadows, climbed wooded hills, and sat on rocks to watch ships out at sea. Constantly they dared each other to carry on stunts which tested their strength and courage. Always they were eager to do scootchers.

Surprise News from Father

WHEN JOHNNIE had attended school a few years, he was ready for grammar school. On the first day he walked slowly up to the front door of the building and peeked inside. There he saw the teacher, Dominie Lyon, standing tall and stern behind his desk. "Come, lad, and take your seat," called the teacher.

Johnnie stepped inside quickly and slipped into a bench at an empty desk. He looked straight ahead but could tell that all the boys were looking at him. Dominie Lyon rapped his rod on the desk and said gruffly, "Everyone in the room get back to work!"

41

Johnnie folded his hands on the desk and quickly stole a look at the other boys. He could see that they looked big and ready for trouble. Already he could tell that he would have a lot of fighting to do.

Johnnie was right in his thinking. Day after day he had to take on any boy his age who dared him to fight. In this way he had to prove himself and his courage to the other boys in the school.

The first month was a very busy one in the grammar school for Johnnie with all his new studies. He had three lessons every day in Latin, three in French, and three in English, as well as one lesson each in geography, history, and arithmetic.

After a few months the boys accepted Johnnie and he didn't have to fight any more. He also pleased his teacher by studying all his lessons well. He was especially interested in reading animal stories from his reading book, *Mac-coulough's Course of Reading.*

One story which he read over and over again in his reader was about a fishhawk and a bald eagle. According to the story, the hawk pulled a fish from the sea. A robber eagle carefully watched what the hawk had done and took after him. The two birds had a fierce air battle, during which the hawk dropped his fish. Then swiftly as a bolt of lightning, the eagle dived down to snatch the falling fish.

Another story which Johnnie liked to read in his reader told about the passenger pigeons in America. These pigeons flew about the country in such great flocks that they darkened the sky like a black cloud.

One long gray afternoon in school, Johnnie turned his head to look out the window at the dark sky. There, stalking across the playground, he saw some boys from a neighboring school. They walked boldly forward, swinging their arms and staring at the building as if looking for trouble. They stood and waited outside.

Quickly Johnnie punched Willie Chisholm, who sat in front of him. "Look outside," he whispered. "The boys from the neighboring school are coming for a fight."

Mr. Lyon heard the whispering and looked over his glasses at Johnnie. "John!" he bellowed. "Stop that whispering!"

"Yes, sir," Johnnie answered quickly and ducked his red head down behind Willie. As he did, though, he stole a quick glance out the window to see more boys marching up the high part of the playground.

By now it was time for school to close. Mr. Lyons looked up at the clock and said, "School is dismissed. All of you go home quietly."

Quickly the boys rushed out of the building. "A fight is on," some of them called.

Cautiously they walked out to face the boys waiting for them. One of the enemy boys stepped out and stood in front of Bob Richardson of the grammar school. "What are you scowling for?" he asked.

Bob took a deep breath. "I'll scowl if I please," he said. "Stop me if you dare!"

"I'll show you whether I dare or not!" replied the intruder as he pulled back his arm and landed a blow squarely on Bob's face, causing him to reel backward.

With this blow the battle started. A big blond boy hit Johnnie on the face and a dull throb went through his cheekbone. Johnnie struck back and tussled with the big boy and finally knocked him down.

The fight went on and on. At last Bob Richardson shouted, "I'll tell you what we'll do. If you'll let us alone, we'll let you alone!" Thus the school war ended.

Wearily Johnnie picked up his books and slung them over his shoulder by the strap. Then he and his friend Willie silently walked toward home together. "We'd better hurry, because we're later than usual getting home," he said. "Our parents will be angry."

As Johnnie hurried along he tried to brush some of the dirt from his clothes. By this time his right eye was beginning to ache and throb. "I hope I don't get a black eye lest I get a thrashing when I reach home," he said.

Willie stopped to look at Johnnie's eye, but he couldn't see much of anything wrong. "It's only a little red and maybe a little puffed up," he said. "Back in the door and maybe no one will notice it."

When Johnnie reached home he was surprised that nobody paid any attention to him. All the members of the family sat at the table listening closely as Father talked about America. He was telling an interesting story about why many Europeans found America a wonderful place to live.

Johnnie sat down at the table and his mother placed a half slice of unbuttered bread and a barley scone on a plate before him. Also, she filled a mug with warm content, a drink made of sweetened milk, and put it beside his plate. As he ate and sipped he listened to his father and in his mind pictured the wonderful land of America.

Regularly after school Johnnie and David went across the street to Grandfather's house to study their lessons for the next day. One winter night in 1849, while they were studying, Father came in with surprising news. "You needn't study your lessons tonight," he said. "We're leaving for America in the morning."

Johnnie's heart pounded with excitement. He couldn't believe that he was really going to

America. At once his mind was filled with thoughts of enchanted American forests, mountains of gold, colorful birds in the sky, and many other exciting things to see. He looked across at David's blue eyes and could tell that his mind was filled with the same exciting thoughts of things to see and do.

Only Grandfather seemed quiet and serious. Johnnie looked into his solemn face and fondly knelt at his knee. "Isn't this news wonderful?" he asked. Then he told his grandfather about the wonderful things he had read and heard about America.

Grandfather pressed a gold coin into each of the boy's hands. "Here are some keepsakes," he said in a low and trembling voice. "Don't expect everything in America to be wonderful. Over there you'll find lessons to study and work to do just as you have here."

Johnnie and David ran back across the street

to their home. On the way they met their friend Willie. "Would you believe we're leaving for America in the morning?" called Johnnie. "We're going there to live."

As soon as Johnnie and David entered the house, Mother said tenderly, "Go right to bed at once, boys. You must get a good night's sleep."

Before the boys left the room Mother explained that Johnnie, David, and Sarah would go to America with their father. The other children would stay in Scotland with her until Father found a home for them in America.

After Johnnie climbed into bed he shivered with delight as he thought how lucky he was to be going to America with Father. He wondered whether he would ever get to sleep, but he was sleeping soundly the next morning when his father shouted, "Come on, boys. It's morning."

First Few Years
in America

BEFORE DAYLIGHT Father, Johnnie, David, and Sarah walked to the railway station to start their trip to America. Johnnie was excited, but he was sad over his tearful parting from the rest of the family. On the train Father told the children about his plans for their future new home in America. Among other things, he told Johnnie and David that he would buy them a pony after they arrived.

At Glasgow they boarded a creaking old sailing vessel to take them across the Atlantic Ocean. It rolled and tossed while it was tied up at the pier. The captain shouted orders and the sailors ran to their posts to start the long journey. Johnnie and David stood on the deck and watched the wind spread the huge sails of the ship.

The voyage across the Atlantic Ocean took over six weeks. During much of this time Sarah and her father were so seasick that they had to stay in their cabin. Johnnie and David, however, scooted about the deck every day, watching the sailors pull ropes and climb the rigging. On calm days when the deck was dry they played games with other boys on the ship.

After Father and the children reached America, he talked with people about different places to live. Many of them recommended Wisconsin, so he decided to go there. A few days later he arrived with the children to set up a new home.

For a few days Father left the children with a neighbor while he built a cabin on the land.

When the little cabin was finished, the neighbor brought the children and their belongings to their new home.

The little cabin was located on a small hill overlooking a meadow covered with spring flowers. Beyond the meadow was a lake fringed with white water lilies. "Does the lake have a name?" asked Johnnie.

Father nodded. "Yes, son, it is called Fountain Lake," he said. "So from now on we'll call our home Fountain Lake Farm."

Johnnie and David ran out to explore the nearby woods and meadows. Soon Johnnie scrambled up a tree and discovered a blue jay's nest containing beautiful green eggs. He reached out to get the eggs but suddenly drew back his hand. "I just can't take these eggs from the nest," he said.

The boys looked about in the woods to find other nests. Soon Johnnie discovered a bluebird's nest in one of the trees. At the same time David called, "Look here. I've found a woodpecker's nest."

Each morning Johnnie and David leaped out of bed with joy to roam barefooted through the meadow and along the edge of the lake. They especially liked to look for frogs, snakes, and turtles in the shallow water.

Just as Father had promised, he bought a pony for the boys. He purchased a little pony from a storekeeper. "Come, lads, to see what I have for you," he called.

When Johnnie saw the pony, he shouted with delight. He ran up and patted his long mane. "How wonderful!" he cried.

David came running right behind Johnnie and asked, "What's his name? Is he really our pony? Does he belong to us?"

"His name is Jack," answered Father, "and you must be good to him."

Jack once had been owned and trained by an Indian. He would stand without being tied. He would come when he was called. He would go anywhere up hill or down, and even jump and swim.

Johnnie and David rode Jack nearly every day. They ran to where he was grazing in the meadow and happily climbed on his back. He took them wherever they wanted to go.

One morning Johnnie threw his arms around Jack's neck and climbed on his bare back. Jack stood perfectly still until Johnnie pressed his heels into his sides. Then he ran over the meadow and the rolling hills with his black mane and tail streaming out in the breeze.

Johnnie was happy with the sun and the summer wind in his face. He galloped along on the pony until they came to the lake, where Jack headed straight for the water. "Whoa, Jack!" Johnnie shouted.

Jack stopped so suddenly that Johnnie flew over the pony's head and landed, sitting upright, at the edge of the lake. He jumped up from the soft wet dirt and brushed off his muddy pants. The pony stood and looked at him as if this was the way a rider always got off his horse. Johnnie laughed and climbed back on Jack and rode off again.

During the coming months, as Johnnie and David roamed about, they found the countryside so exciting and wonderful that they could hardly believe their eyes. They saw carpets of wild flowers on the ground. They saw colorful birds and hundreds of flying insects they had never seen before.

One of the most unbelievable sights of all was Fountain Lake Meadow dotted with millions of lightning bugs. Suddenly one summer evening when Johnnie noticed the meadow glowing with light, he thought there must be something wrong with his eyes. "Davey! Davey!" he called. "Do you see anything strange in the meadow?"

David looked and shook his head in disbelief. "Yes, it's all covered with shaky fire-sparks," he cried.

Yankee, the hired man, overheard the boys talking and started to laugh. "Oh, they're nothing but lightning bugs," he said. He took the boys down the hill to the meadow. With a swoop of his hand he caught several lightning bugs for each of them. Then the boys walked gleefully back to the house with the little flashing bugs cupped in their hands.

Inside the house the boys dropped the little bugs one by one into a glass jar. That night after they went to bed they watched the strange little lights go on and off. "How pretty they are!" they cried.

One day when Johnnie was outdoors he noticed that the air was heavy and hard to breathe. He looked up and saw dark clouds mounting in the sky. Just then Yankee walked up, also looking at the sky. "We're going to have a heavy thunderstorm before long," he said. "We probably should look for some kind of shelter."

Soon the sky was filled with thunder and lightning. Next rain came pelting down. Johnnie was pleased. He liked wild storms.

It was too far to run to the house, so he and Yankee crawled under bushes. Johnnie's heart pounded with excitement as thunder and lightning split the air. Suddenly the lightning hit an old oak tree across the woods and it burst into flames. It looked as if the whole world might be set afire.

Soon the furious storm moved on. The punky old oak tree burned itself out, but the rest of the woods was too wet to catch fire.

Johnnie and Yankee went to watch the tree burn. By this time the old tree merely lay smoldering on the ground.

Often the Muir children saw thin blue smoke curling up from tepees in an Indian village on the other side of Fountain Lake. These Indians were poor but not warlike. One day Sarah saw an Indian sharpening a knife on the grindstone outside the cabin. Moments later she trembled with fear as he came to the door. "Pork flour," he grunted.

Sarah quickly shoved a piece of pork through the door. The Indian grabbed the food and started to walk away. Johnnie and David came running up just in time to see him walking down the hill. Sarah stood on the steps wringing her hands. "What's the matter, Sarah?" Johnnie shouted.

"An Indian was just here," she whispered. "I'm still a little scared."

The boys looked back just in time to see the Indian paddling off to the village across the lake. To them he didn't look scary at all.

Each day Father, Yankee, and the boys went out to cut and burn trees and bushes so they could plow the land. All of them worked very hard from morning to night. Later they planted corn and other crops on the land.

Besides clearing the land and planting crops, they built a frame house on the hill. In the fall when the house was finished, Father sent for Mother and the other children to come from Scotland. Then with Mother, Margaret, little Daniel, and the three-year-old twins, Mary and Annie, at home, the house was filled with joy and laughter.

That first winter for the Muir family in Wisconsin was extremely hard and cold. The only heat for the entire house came from the kitchen stove. In bitter zero weather all members of the family shivered around the stove. Some nights their socks and boots even froze solidly placed nearby.

Otherwise the Muirs greatly enjoyed tho Wisconsin winter. The stars were so bright that the whole family gazed and gazed as if they had never seen stars before. They also enjoyed the snowstorms with the crystal flakes falling one by one. They even enjoyed wading in snowdrifts several feet deep.

Following the cold winter, Father, Yankee, and the boys started the spring plowing for planting crops. Johnnie liked to plant the corn, wheat, and potatoes. He found the spring of the year a happy time. The birds sang merrily, and rich green colors covered the meadows and the trees.

With summer came the very heavy work of hoeing and weeding crops. There were animals to be fed, scythes to be sharpened, and stovewood to be chopped. Water had to be carried up the hill from a spring.

There was so much to be done that even the girls helped. Margaret helped Johnnie to harvest the grain. As he swung the cradle to cut the stalks, she tied them into bundles.

On other days both the boys and girls worked in the hayfield from morning till night. After supper they had their evening chores to do. Finally Father held a family worship and all the children tumbled into bed.

Johnnie discovered that there was always work to do on the farm, both in winter and summer. He felt sad and wished that he could run across the street to see his grandfather and grandmother back in Scotland. He thought of what Grandfather had said, "You'll find there'll be a lot of hard work in America."

From Farm Life to College

AFTER A FEW YEARS, the family bought and moved to a larger farm, called Hickory Hill Farm. Johnnie and all the other children worked hard to help clear the land. Later they toiled from morning to night plowing, planting, and harvesting crops in the new fields. They cut down trees to obtain wood for building fences and to use for fuel. Morning and evening they did a variety of chores, which included taking care of the horses, cattle, hogs, and other farm animals.

Hickory Hill Farm was high and dry without any springs or streams for securing water. Father tried to blast out a well in the rocky ground but couldn't break a hole through the rocks. Finally he decided this work had to be done by hand with a hammer and chisel. Since Johnnie was the oldest boy in the family, he was selected to do most of the work.

Each morning Father and David lowered Johnnie in a bucket to the bottom of the well where he hammered and chiseled all day long to break away pieces of rock. He worked in murky darkness and his only light came from the opening in the ground above him. As he chiseled his way deeper and deeper he could scarcely see the light of day.

One morning when Father and David lowered Johnnie to the bottom of the well, he suddenly began to feel dizzy. He couldn't pick up his tools to start working. Father called, "What's keeping you so still down there, Johnnie? Say something to me."

Johnnie tried to answer but couldn't make his father hear. At last he managed feebly to call, "Get me out of here. Somehow I can't breathe or move."

At once Father knew that a dangerous gas, called carbon dioxide, had settled in the bottom of the well. He realized that this gas was extremely dangerous and that he must get Johnnie out as quickly as possible. "Climb into the bucket, Johnnie, and hold on," he shouted nervously.

Johnnie tried several times and finally managed to crawl into the bucket. Then Father hoisted him to the top of the well and pulled him out into the fresh air. There he sprawled on the ground and gasped for breath.

After a few days, the carbon dioxide cleared out of the well, and once more Johnnie could return to work. Suddenly, one day, a strong gush of water poured into the bottom of the well. Now he realized that he had reached water and that his tedious hammering and chiseling work was ended at last.

Johnnie's tasks were so many that he had little opportunity to read or study books. He was eager to read some of the books he had brought from Scotland and others which he had borrowed from friends. The only time he could read and study, however, was in the evening after he had finished his work. Sometimes he even fell asleep while he was reading.

Usually Johnnie sat at the kitchen table to read by the light of a candle. This was the only time he could find to be alone with books. One night when he was absorbed in the midst of a story his father called, "Johnnie, stop reading at once and go to bed. From now on you must go to bed when the rest of us do."

Father's orders came as a great shock to Johnnie. Just as he started to blow out the candle his father called again and said, "From now on you must do all your reading in the morning. You may get up as early as you like to read, but be careful not to disturb the rest of us."

The next morning Johnnie awoke at one o'clock. He could scarcely believe his eyes when he held his candle before the clock to see what time it was. Now he would have five full hours to read and study before starting his day's work on the farm.

He went to the cellar where he wouldn't disturb anybody, but soon found it was too chilly for him to sit still and read. Now he decided to spend his time working on a model of a new type of sawmill which he had planned. Several mornings he awakened early and continued to work on the model until it was finished.

After he finished working on his sawmill model, he tested it in a stream in a nearby meadow. Besides a sawmill he made models of many other things, including water hygrometers, pyrometers, and a barometer. One of his most interesting models was a clock which not only struck and showed time but lit a fire and a lamp and even tipped a bed on end to get a person up. He called this invention his "early rising machine."

The Muirs' neighbors and friends all talked about Johnnie's clock and other interesting models. During the summer they suggested that he exhibit them at the Wisconsin State Agricultural Fair to be held a few weeks later at Madison, the state capital. Johnnie shook his head at the suggestion. "Who would want to look at such simple things, most of which I have shaped crudely out of wood?" he asked. 'Why would anyone want to see them?"

"The fact that they're made of wood doesn't make any difference," replied his friends. "The important thing is that you have thought of them and made them. People will think of you as a sort of inventor."

Johnnie found that many people were interested in his exhibits at the State Agricultural Fair. Numerous ladies and gentlemen strolled through the building and stopped to watch him demonstrate his models. They were especially amused to see what happened when the son of Professor Ezra Carr, geology professor at the University of Wisconsin, offered to demonstrate how Johnnie's "early rising machine" worked. The little boy lay down on the bed and Johnnie explained what would happen as he set the clock. Right on time the bed rose up quickly and threw the boy out standing upright on his feet. Everyone clapped wildly in amusement.

The newspapers heard about the interesting models which Johnnie had created and was exhibiting at the fair. They sent reporters to look at his exhibits and to talk with him about them. They carried stories about him and some of the ingenious things he had devised and made into simple models.

From the fairgrounds Johnnie could see the University of Wisconsin among the hills in the distance. Each day after the exhibit closed he strolled through the University campus, looking at buildings and thinking of things he still wanted to learn. He felt an almost uncontrollable yearning to start back to school again.

Briefly he worked to earn money and in 1860 he enrolled as a student at the University. He started to specialize in natural sciences, which provided background for his future career. He was especially interested in geology, which told the story of changes and conditions on the surface of the earth.

Fortunately, Johnnie's geology professor was

Dr. Ezra Carr, whose son had helped him demonstrate his "early rising machine" at the State Agricultural Fair. Dr. Carr often took Johnnie home with him, where he became a close friend of the family. Through Dr. Carr Johnnie became still more interested in geology. Often the professor took him and his other students on hikes along lake shores and among the hills to study. He recommended many books about glaciers and other subjects which Johnnie devoured from cover to cover.

At the University, Johnnie met many professors and others who were interested in conserving trees and other natural resources. He read many books on the subject and felt that drastic steps should be taken to halt the terrible destruction of forests that was taking place. This destruction later would lead to a scarcity of lumber and the loss of many forms of wild life.

One day Johnnie and two of his friends, one of whom was deeply interested in botany, stood under a huge locust tree on the campus. The botany student reached up and pulled down a locust blossom and pointed to its parts. "See how closely this locust flower looks like the flower of the pea," he said.

The third boy paid little attention to what the botany student said, but Johnnie listened closely. He already was strongly interested in botany. The next Sunday he joined his botany friend in identifying and pressing plants. They carefully examined each plant and located its name in a reference table at the end of a book. Johnnie was thrilled. "That's wonderful!" he exclaimed. "I'll get a botany book and we can go looking for plants together."

Johnnie had always liked flowers, but now he had a new reason for enjoying them. The next week he bought a botany book and this was the beginning of his lifelong study of plantlife and what it means to the world. As a young man, he was fast becoming a nature lover, who found both comfort and joy in the great outdoors. He was not only interested in plants but in all the wonders of nature.

74

A Long Hike

AFTER SPENDING two and one-half years at the University of Wisconsin, young John Muir felt the urge to set out to explore the world of nature. Even though he left the University with great sadness, he felt that he was only joining the larger university of the wilderness. People no longer called him Johnnie. Now they thought of him as a serious-minded student of the great outdoors.

With the first sign of spring he left home with a light pack on his back to start his explorations. He hiked all the way across Michigan to Lake Superior and on into Canada. Each night he slept under the stars and each day he lived on fish which he caught from lakes and streams, and on berries and other fruits which he picked from trees and shrubs.

From Canada he traveled southward, and by September reached Niagara Falls, where he was joined by his younger brother Danny. The two brothers stayed at Niagara Falls for a week and had exciting times together. They stood for hours and watched the gigantic waterfalls and listened to their thunderous roar.

The following year Muir worked in a machine shop in Canada which manufactured broom handles. During the year the factory burned down and the owners offered to take him in as a partner after the factory could be rebuilt. He refused by saying that he didn't want to work in a factory that depended on cutting down trees.

From Canada young Muir traveled by train

to Indianapolis, Indiana, where he obtained a job in a machine shop. He chose Indianapolis because there still were numerous forests nearby where he could roam and study. Even though he had to work to earn money, he still was most interested in exploring the wilderness to find out more about nature.

At Indianapolis Muir was a clever and successful mechanic, but found time to do much reading about faraway places he would like to visit. He read about the magnificent Yosemite Valley and the majestic Sierra Nevada in California, and about spectacular places to visit in different parts of South America. At night he even dreamed about some of the sights he wanted to see.

One day as he worked at his bench in the factory, a file suddenly flew from his hand and hit his right eye. He clutched his injured eye with his hand and stumbled over to the nearby window. When he removed his hand, he discovered that the sight in this eye was completely gone. In horror, he exclaimed, "I've lost the sight of one eye!"

For a week he lay in the hospital with his right eye heavily bandaged. At first the doctor predicted that he would never see out of this eye again. Sadly, Muir turned his face to the wall and said, "Now I'll never be able to see all the wonderful things in nature that I had hoped to see during my lifetime."

Later a specialist examined his eye and decided that he could, with medication and care, regain much of the vision he had lost. The doctor explained, "You'll have to remain in a dark room for four weeks, but afterward you'll be able to see almost as well as ever."

"Oh, how wonderful!" cried Muir.

The world never looked more beautiful to him as he gradually regained his sight. Each day he could see more and more about him as objects came out of the darkness. Day after day the owners of the machine shop visited him to talk about his early return to work. He listened courteously, but in the back of his mind he was still dreaming of exploring faraway, interesting parts of the world.

On a bright sunny day in April, soon after he left the hospital, he took a stroll in a nearby woods. With rays of sunlight streaming through the trees, he found the woods refreshingly green and beautiful. At once he realized that he could never return to work in the machine shop as long as he could visit wonderful places like this.

He returned to Wisconsin to visit his parents and the other members of his family. While there he revisited some of the forests, hills, valleys, streams, and lakes which he had loved as a growing boy. Somehow, he was already forming in his mind the idea that many of the wonders of nature in America should be preserved as national parks which people would be free to visit and enjoy.

His father couldn't understand his special love of nature and felt that he should settle down again to hard work on the farm. When he left, however, his elder sister Sarah called after him, "You know, John, we expect great things of you."

In September, 1867, young Muir boarded a train in Indianapolis and traveled to Jeffersonville, Indiana, across the Ohio River from Louisville, Kentucky. He crossed the river on a ferry boat and started a one-thousand mile walk to the Gulf of Mexico. Carrying only a little bag of personal belongings and a frame for preserving and pressing plants, he hurried through the streets of Louisville to reach the open country. There he started to walk happily along dusty roads, realizing that the great out-doors was the right place for him.

One after another, as he walked through Kentucky, he saw hills and valleys, grand forests and scattered fields of corn, tobacco, and cotton. For the first time in his life he saw mistletoe hanging from the limbs of trees. He visited both Horse Cave and Mammoth Cave and marveled at their grandeur. He stopped only long enough to sleep at night and to eat simple meals during the day.

He traveled mostly through the woods. He only took to the roads when it was necessary to reach where he wanted to go. When he came to the Cumberland Mountains between Tennessee and North Carolina, he was especially thrilled because these were the first real mountains he had ever seen. As he stood on top of the mountains and looked down into the valleys below, he felt that the scenery here was grander than he had ever witnessed before in any of his travels.

For weeks Muir tramped southward through North Carolina into Georgia. He traveled slowly in order to study trees, plants, and flowers along the way. Each night when he lay down to sleep under the branches of a tree, he felt extremely fortunate to have the whole world for his bedroom.

While Muir was in Georgia, a friend took him for a ride in a rowboat on the Chattahoochee River. As they rowed slowly along the banks of the river, he reached up and picked wild grapes from grapevines in trees overhanging the water. Then he sat at one end of the rowboat and munched the wild grapes as if he had discovered the land of plenty.

As Muir left to continue his journey, his friend cautioned him to watch for rattlesnakes in the warm summer climate. "This is the time of year for them to come out of hiding, so beware," he warned.

Muir listened to his friend's warning but said nothing. He merely picked up his things and set out across the field. He hoped that having to watch for rattlesnakes wouldn't interfere with his enjoyment of nature.

First he needed to cross the river in order to continue southward. The vines and other plants in the thicket along the banks of the river were so tangled that he could barely work his way through. Finally he stepped into the water, planning to wade and swim across to the other side.

When he was about halfway across the river, a swift current caught him and carried him downstream. He kicked with his feed and paddled with one arm to guide himself and held his little bag above water with his other arm. Pounding and beating the water, he feverishly struggled to free himself from the strong current. Fortunately he soon came to a shallow spot where he grabbed on to a projecting rock. There he hung on tightly until he could regain his strength. Then he crept out to a level spot

where he stretched out to rest and dry himself in the hot southern sun.

As he continued his journey, he walked through low sandy country, covered with tall grasses and dense forests with Spanish moss hanging from most of the oak trees. Each day he came across birds and trees that he had never seen before. For the first time in his life he felt as if he were traveling in a strange country.

The nights were especially lonely and frightening for him in his strange surroundings. The forests were so dark that he could scarcely move about safely and the wind filled the air with eerie sounds. One night he tried to bathe in a still dark stream, ever fearful that he would come across a rattlesnake or an alligator. Suddenly he caught sight of a light in a nearby farmhouse and started to walk toward it as a means of protection. Fortunately, the family in the house took him in and made him welcome for the rest of the night.

By now young Muir had reached the southern coast of Georgia and was ready to cross over into Florida. He was eager to reach Florida, because he knew he would find many tropical plants there which he had never seen before. Within a few days he trudged through marshy swamps, examined one flowering plant after another, and admired the beautiful palm trees towering overhead. Each night he slept wherever he could find a bit of dry ground rising above the swamps. Each day he ate at campfires where he mingled with all sorts of persons traveling about the country, some of whom were even outlaws.

When Muir reached Cedar Keys, on the Gulf of Mexico, he decided to stop and work for a while to earn some money. He wanted to earn enough money to travel by ship to other countries to continue his study of tropical plants. He obtained a job at a sawmill located along the harbor, but after a few days collapsed from an attack of malarial fever. The owner of the mill where he worked took him home with him. There the owner's wife nursed him through a very serious illness, which otherwise might have cost him his life.

After Muir partially recovered, he traveled on a ship loaded with lumber to Havana, Cuba. Each day he sauntered through the streets of the city, and each night he slept on board the ship. He enjoyed the sights and sounds of the city, but he was still too weak from his illness to continue his study of tropical plants. His attacks of malaria kept recurring, and he felt that he should return northward to a cooler climate for a while.

Soon he traveled to New York on a ship loaded with oranges. There he stayed until he could throw off the malaria which long had been plaguing him. Then he decided to go to California to continue his study of nature. All of his life this had been one of his fondest hopes and dreams. In New York he boarded a steamer which took him to the Isthmus of Panama. There he traveled overland to the Pacific Ocean, where he boarded another steamer which took him to San Francisco. He arrived in March, 1868, eager to explore this new and different part of the United States.

Explorations
in Yosemite

IN MARCH, 1868, when Muir stepped on the wharf at San Francisco, he was greeted by a sharp wind which struck him in the face. This sharp wind made him feel chilly and ruffled his long hair and beard. He looked about him and could hardly wait to see the wonders of California. "At last I am here!" he exclaimed.

He walked along the noisy wharf and soon came to Market Street, one of the leading streets in the city. He pushed his way along the crowded sidewalks, and his feet grew tired from walking. He was disappointed and eager to reach the open country as soon as possible.

San Francisco was not what he had come to California to see. He wanted to see mountains, forests, valleys, waterfalls, and streams. Finally he stopped a man coming down the street and asked, "Mister, what is the quickest way to get out of town?"

The man looked at him in surprise. "Where do you want to go?" he asked.

"Anywhere to reach the wide open country," replied Muir.

The man looked at Muir's rumpled, shabby clothes, his long hair and beard, and his piercing blue eyes. He backed off a few steps and said, "You'd better take the ferry across San Francisco Bay to Oakland and then walk a few blocks eastward in Oakland and you'll come to open country."

Muir carefully followed the man's directions and crossed the bay to Oakland. Then on the first day of April he set out for Yosemite, start-

90

ing with an exciting walk through the Santa Clara Valley. The valley was bathed in sunshine and the hills were covered with brilliantly colored flowers. The songs of meadowlarks filled the air.

He climbed into the highlands east of the Santa Clara Valley until he came to a pass. From there he looked down on the most beautiful sight he had ever seen. Before him lay the great Central Valley of California, spreading out like a glorious lake of golden sunshine. The whole valley seemed to be a vast bed of colorful flowers.

To the east of the Central Valley, he could see the foothills of the high Sierra Nevada, or Snowy Mountains, as the Spaniards called them. As he caught a glimpse of the mountains far in the distance, their snowy peaks gleamed softly under the bright spring sun. His view of these mountains glistening in the sunlight led him to feel that they should have been called the "Range of Light."

After traveling for several days, Muir finally came to Yosemite. As he approached he was awestruck by the beauty of the great canyon. He found it surrounded by granite walls with sunlight coming in from above. Its grandeur made him feel as if he were in a great temple. For days he traveled about, exploring and feeling the beauty of the mountains, the tumbling waterfalls, the trees, and the flowers. To him it seemed that every part of nature was grander in Yosemite than he had found in any other part of the world.

When he finished his exploration he returned to the great Central Valley of California to find work in the harvest fields. He felt strong and refreshed from traveling through the mountains and drinking clear crystal water. Fortunately, he readily found a job and worked hard until the harvest was over. Every day, however, he greatly missed the mountains.

After the harvest he turned to other kinds of work, including riding and breaking wild Arabian horses. He was a careful rider and rode the bucking horses as skillfully as any of the caballeros. Happily he yelled and laughed as he rode with one hand holding the reins and the other hand held high over his head.

Later he worked as a sheepherder. He and other sheepherders took flocks of sheep high up into the mountains to graze. As he climbed through the mountains he felt more joyful than he had ever felt before.

One day as he was strolling a short distance from camp he noticed that some of the boulders on the mountain slopes were different in color from the granite of the mountains themselves. He observed that they were a different kind of rock, as if they did not belong there.

Suddenly it came to him that these boulders had been carried down by a glacier. "They have been brought here on an ice sheet," he cried. "This whole area has been carved out by a glacier. I have made an important discovery here."

During the late summer and fall he tried to see as many of the wonders of nature in the highlands as possible. One day, while exploring, he stood at the top of a waterfall and watched the noisy rushing water hurtling down. He wondered how it would seem to look through that falling water.

Without thinking, he took off his shoes and socks and crawled down the rock alongside the falling water. As he lowered himself, he found the pounding, roaring water beside him very exciting. He slipped his body down as far as he could go safely. Then he sat back and clung to the polished rock to admire the falls.

From this position, he saw a tiny ledge below him with just enough room for his heels. Slowly and cautiously he moved on down to this ledge, where he could look directly into the streaming, frothy water of the falls. He never knew how he managed to climb back to the top of the falls in safety.

For weeks as a sheepherder, Muir reveled in the beauty and wonder of nature in Yosemite. Day after day he climbed the mountains and looked down at the splendors of the valleys. More and more he could see how all forms of nature work together.

Every day his explorations made clear to him his theory of glaciers cutting out the valleys. He could see the shining surfaces of rocks in the mountain walls, polished smooth by glaciers. He could see how the glaciers had created the curved forms of valleys and flowed into the crevasses of the mountains. He could see how lakes and meadows were located where the deepest parts of glaciers had been.

Later he wrote to explain his great happiness from living and studying in the mountains. "How interesting everything is," he wrote. "Every rock, mountain, stream, plant, lake, forest, garden, bird, beast, insect seems to call us to come and learn something of its history and relationship."

During the fall Muir and the other sheepherders took the sheep back down to the Central Valley for the winter. He worked for a while on a ranch but soon realized that he had to return to the Yosemite and the mountains. Another worker on the ranch and close friend of his, Harry Randall, decided to go with him.

When Muir and Randall reached Yosemite, they applied for jobs at the Upper Hotel on the bank of the Merced River. "I happen to need a couple of men," said James Hutchings, the owner of the hotel. "You'll have to milk cows, drive oxen, and cut and haul logs."

Randall started to say that he didn't know how to do any of these things, but Muir punched him in the ribs to be still. "We'll be glad to take the jobs and work hard for you," he said boldly.

That night Muir and Randall camped in the valley only a short distance from the hotel. As they sat beside their campfire, they noticed a shadow approaching in the darkness. Soon they realized that the approaching figure was Mr. Hutchings. "Hello," he called. "Do either of you know anything about sawmills?"

"Yes, I am a millwright by trade," answered Muir, explaining about the earlier sawmill work that he had done.

"I need a good deal of sawed lumber to build cottages and repair the hotel," explained Mr. Hutchings. "Will you come to look at my saw-

mill to find out what's wrong with it and see whether or not you can make it work?"

The next day Muir went to look over the sawmill, which was run by a waterwheel in a stream. He examined both the sawmill and the waterwheel and found them badly damaged. Then he explained that they would have to be repaired to make them work properly. "Will you take on the job of repairing them and then cutting the lumber?" asked Mr. Hutchings. "I will pay you $90 a month and provide you with a place to sleep and your meals."

Muir agreed to take the job if he could get the lumber from already fallen trees. "You won't have to cut any trees," said Mr. Hutchings, "because more than a hundred trees were uprooted recently in a storm. They'll provide all the lumber I will need and more, too."

The next day Muir and Randall started to build a cabin made out of fallen sugar pine trees. They laid rock slabs for the floor wide enough apart so that ferns could grow up through the cracks. They dug a channel so that a little creek would flow through a corner of the cabin. In one wall they built a fireplace, and in another wall they built a window facing Yosemite Falls.

Inside the cabin Muir made a rough wooden desk with an arch of green plants above it. He and Randall slept in hammocks hung from the ceiling so that they could see Yosemite Falls through the window. Each night they lay watching the trembling frothy water and listening to the low sweet tones of the little creek rippling through the cabin.

After Muir and Randall were settled in their cabin, Muir repaired the sawmill and waterwheel. Then they sawed up the lumber from the fallen trees which Mr. Hutchings had wanted. Each day they worked from morning

100

to night bringing logs to the mill and sawing them into boards and other kinds of lumber.

When the heavy storms came and stopped them from working, Muir rushed out to enjoy the winter beauty. He spent every day outdoors and sometimes all night, wandering, climbing, and studying everything he could see or hear. He loved to be alone with nature.

Early each morning Muir was startled by booming noises echoing and reechoing through the valley. He wondered what caused these thunderlike sounds. At last he discovered that the sounds were caused by big chunks of ice falling from cliffs along the falls. The morning sun warmed the valley and melted ice that had formed during the night.

The winter was especially colorful in the mountains and valleys. During the day the sun poured down over the white snowy domes and glistening rocks. During the night the silvery moon and twinkling stars set everything about the cabin aglow in shadowy forms.

One bright sunny morning after a snowfall of three or four feet, Muir set out to climb a ridge high above the valley. He hoped to reach the top by evening to see the sunset, but found climbing slow and difficult. When evening came he was still far from the top. Pausing briefly, he stared on up the mountain in despair.

Suddenly as he was looking about the snow gave way and he started to fall. He threw himself on his back and spread out his arms and legs. Then he rode the avalanche of snow like a flash nearly three thousand feet to the bottom of the canyon. When the avalanche came to rest, he was on top of the pile of ice and snow without having suffered a bruise. He could scarcely realize what had happened.

In the spring visitors started to come to Yosemite and Muir was called upon to act as a guide. In the meantime, Dr. Ezra Carr, his former professor at the University of Wisconsin, had moved to the University of California. When Mrs. Carr learned that Muir was at Yosemite she sent many visitors to ask for him to serve as their guide.

As Muir guided the tourists he told them how he believed glaciers had once cut their way through the rocks to form valleys. Many people, including the state geologist, disagreed with his theory. The geologist didn't think his idea was even worth talking about.

In late summer of 1870 a geology professor and group of students from the University of California came to Yosemite on a camping trip. They explored the mountains and valleys of the park carefully with Muir as their guide. As he led the group, he pointed out evidences here and there of his glacial theory. All the visitors were greatly interested.

On the second night they camped beside a mountain lake. After supper Muir and the professor went down to sit on a rock overlooking the lake. They were so overcome with the beauty of the glittering moonlight on the water that they sat for an hour or so without saying a word.

On the succeeding days they climbed to the summit of Mount Dana. As they stood at this high point they looked down at the river valley below. Immediately the professor looked at John and agreed that the valleys had been carved out by glaciers. John smiled, glad to have this professor agree with him.

In the Mountains

FROM NOW ON Muir constantly watched for the proof of icy glaciers on the mountains and in the valleys. He hiked through rocky canyons and past frothy waterfalls. He tramped through green meadows and beside cold mountain lakes. He walked up the rocky river beds of tumbling mountain streams. He looked sharply at each perfect flower and bush and tree. He was fascinated by the order of all nature's parts, animals, growing plants and trees, rocks, streams, waterfalls, and mountains.

In searching for clues to prove his glacial theory, he looked carefully at each mountain rock and boulder. He measured heights and widths with great care. No unusual stripe or mark on a rock escaped his keen eye.

At night he slept under the stars. When the sun started to slip behind the canyon walls, he made his camp for the night. Usually he gathered wood chips and brown needles which had fallen from the pine trees to start a fire. He placed twigs and dry logs on top for firewood. Then when he lit the fire, the wood chips and needles crackled loudly and ignited the logs.

He dipped water from a rushing mountain stream and placed a dipper of water over the coals. He reached in his pocket, took out a few tea leaves, and put them in a tin cup. Then he poured the boiling water in the cup to make tea. Finally he sat down by the crackling fire and reached in his pocket and pulled out a crust of dry bread.

Regularly he sat with his back against a tree

and his feet toward the fire. He sipped his tea
and munched his bread by firelight. He felt
fortunate to have the entire canyon as his din-
ing table with beautiful surroundings.

The tall straight fir trees around the campsite reached toward the stars twinkling in the dark sky. The night was filled with the small noises coming from the forest. The sound of the mountain waters rushing over the falls and dropping to the bottom of the canyon provided a continuous musical background.

Muir sat by the campfire quietly, enjoying the beautiful sights and sounds around him. He sat up straight to breathe deeply of the fresh mountain air. The dark, velvety night enfolded him like a rich cloak.

While sitting by the campfire, he thought of how well all wild things were cared for in nature. He thought about birds with their smooth, oily feathers, beetles with their hard shiny shells, and bears with their shaggy, heavy fur coats. He thought of squirrels having warm socks and mittens and tails wide enough to use for blankets. He thought of wild sheep with overcoats of oily wool to protect them from snow and icy rain during the winter.

Later a frown spread over Muir's face. Even though he was content and happy, he felt a small feeling of sadness deep inside him. He started to think about his family and friends. One by one, he thought of his sisters and brothers, all of whom were married and leading useful lives. Likewise all of his friends were married and settled down.

He looked down at the ground and thought about himself. He wasn't married and didn't have a home. He didn't even earn a living. Thoughtfully he shook his head. Perhaps he should go into the city and take a job. He looked at his strong hands and knew he could work with machinery again just as he had done some years before.

The thought of working in a factory again made him shudder. He would feel trapped if he couldn't wander in the mountains. His frown grew deeper as he pondered what good he would do by working in a city.

For many minutes he sat and gazed into the flickering firelight of the campfire. He looked at the beauties of the forest around him. He felt hypnotized by the smell of the fir trees and the sounds of the forest. Suddenly the answer came to him. He knew that he couldn't leave to go to a city. He had to remain in the mountains. Besides, he still wanted to prove that valleys and canyons had been shaped and formed by glaciers.

At last he lay down by the fire to sleep. He felt good with his decision, knowing that in the life he had chosen he would always enjoy the music of waterfalls, whistling winds, and singing birds. He could study the rocks and learn the effects of landslides and avalanches. He would know the trees and flowers, and he could share what he learned and his love of nature with others who might be interested.

One Sunday morning before long Muir found proof that Yosemite had been formed by a glacier. He discovered a narrow wedge in the rocks where ice had pushed through and had hardened and grooved the granite in its path. Then he traced glacial material everywhere as he followed Yosemite Creek to its source. He was even able to map out the length and width of the glacier. He also could see the route this enormous river of ice had taken.

Many of Muir's friends, including Mrs. Carr, urged him to write about his discoveries in Yosemite. He welcomed this suggestion but was uneasy about writing articles for scholars and scientists to read. In the back of his mind, however, he realized that he had many important facts to reveal about nature.

Finally a noted scientist from the East came

to Yosemite to study Muir's glacial findings. He was convinced that Muir's theory was right. As he left he said, "You must write about your findings to keep us scientists informed."

Following this invitation Muir decided to come down from the mountains for a while to write. He wrote an article about his search for a prehistoric glacier in Yosemite. His article, "The Death of a Glacier," was published in the *New York Tribune.*

That fall he again renewed his explorations to find traces of the lost glacier. One day in October when he was exploring between two mountain ranges, he found a little stream of gray glacial mud. At once he fell to his knees to examine the mud with his hands. "There's no doubt!" he shouted. "This is glacial mud. I've found a living glacier here!"

Breathlessly he climbed up higher and saw his first living glacier, flowing down from the cliffs of Black Mountain. "Now I have a real story to tell!" he exclaimed.

At this time many scientists and artists were coming to California to study Yosemite and other mountain valleys. One day three of the artists asked Muir to guide them on a tour through the mountains. Muir agreed and enjoyed acting as their guide. He was surprised and delighted to learn that they were all Scotsmen. "There's nobody like a Scotsman to see beauty in the world around him," he said.

When Muir and the artists started along the trail Muir discovered that he and one of them, William Keith, had been born in Scotland the same year. Feeling like long-lost brothers, the two became friends for life. At once they started to call each other by their first names. "Johnnie," said Keith, "do you know of any mountain scenery that would make a good picture? If so, take me there."

"I know just the place, Willie," said Muir, delighted. "It looks like a picture hanging from the sky."

On horseback he led the artists along a brightly sunlit mountain path. As they came round a bend and faced a cluster of snow-topped peaks, he pulled in his horse and waited. He was eager to see the faces of the others when they first saw the beautiful view before them.

The scene was perfect. Great towering snowcapped peaks jutted into the blue sky. The valley below glowed with red, purple, and golden sunshine. As an added touch, a lively mountain stream tumbled through the meadow.

The artists were stunned by the overpowering beauty of the scene. They climbed silently from their horses and stared as if they couldn't look long or hard enough. Then, as soon as they could get their supplies together, they started sketching the unusual scene before them.

The next morning Muir left the artists to go out mountaineering on his own. He wanted to climb Mount Ritter, which he called the "King of the mid-Sierras." At that time no one had ever climbed to the top of this peak.

That night he camped in a valley and the next morning started to climb a long slope of the mountain. On the way up, he had to cross a glacier. Climbing carefully, he began to zig-zag up an ice-covered cliff. He found it harder and harder to find a foothold.

Suddenly he was stopped with no way to go. He could see no cracks or seams to hang on to. He could move neither his hands nor his feet. With his arms outstretched, all he could do was cling to the sharp surface of the ice.

Feeling helpless, he began to panic. He stole a look at the ice far below and panicked even more. He knew that if he fell he would never be seen again. What could he do? He couldn't think of any way to help himself.

Briefly he hung there. His body was covered with cold sweat. His heart pounded, but he took a deep breath and all at once began to think calmly again. With sharp eyes he looked for the slightest little dent in the rock.

Miraculously, he managed to scale the icy wall. Bit by bit he scratched and crawled until he came to a safe resting place. There he sprawled out breathless and slowly regained his strength. As he rested in the warm sunlight he felt filled with renewed courage. After a short rest, he got to his feet and started on toward the top of the mountain.

Slowly he climbed up through the rough black rocks to the top. To the east he saw a barren desert, and to the south, slopes that led down to the valley of the San Joaquin River.

The sun was low when he started back down the mountain. Slowly and carefully he made his way down until he reached his campsite. Then he dropped to the ground and slept soundly for several hours.

While Keith and the other artists worked in the valley, Muir made several other mountain hikes by himself. When he returned from his last trip, the artists invited him to go back to San Francisco with them. He accepted their invitation, but he stayed only two weeks. Although he met many interesting people while he was in San Francisco, he could hardly wait to get back to the mountains.

That winter Muir took time to write several articles for magazines and newspapers. In these articles he told of his most recent discoveries. When spring came, however, the mountains called him and he started out to explore the entire length of the Sierra Nevada.

A new John Muir was about to emerge. Up to now he had spent all his life chiefly as a naturalist. Soon he was to become interested in safeguarding nature, and would start a career as a conservationist.

In this career he would work to save the wonders of nature from needless destruction by man. Already he was becoming alarmed by how rapidly lumbering companies, mining companies, and others were ruining the great outdoors by their wasteful activities.

More Climbing and Writing

"THE MOUNTAINS are calling me and I must go," said Muir as he set out to explore the entire length of the Sierra Nevada. On this long and exciting adventure he was joined by three close friends, including a famous botanist and a well-known artist.

Muir climbed up mountain after mountain to seek out the wondrous works of nature. He gloried in the view of the whole mountain scenery. He delighted in the beauty of all the different kinds of trees. He spent nearly a week tramping through the sequoia forests south of Kings Canyon. When he saw Kings Canyon, he thought that it contained the most beautiful mountain scenery in America. Time and again he had to pause briefly to rest or to catch his breath.

He left his companions in camp and set out to climb Mount Whitney, the highest mountain in the nation outside Alaska. In his pocket he carried a map to guide him. The wind blew cold as he climbed up the jagged rocks and through the snow to reach the top.

When he reached the summit, he stood up breathlessly to look about him. He saw the tops of several other mountains and the valleys between them. To the north he saw another mountain at least five hundred feet higher than the mountain he was on. With difficulty in the high wind, he spread out his map to find Mount Whitney, and there it was. The mountain on which he stood was marked Mount Whitney on the map, highest in the

Sierra range, but the map was wrong. Discovering the mistake, he set out for the real Mount Whitney.

Muir struggled up the difficult climb of the real Mount Whitney. He grew colder and colder until his hands and feet were numb with the freezing cold. His face and beard were stiff with frozen bits of moisture.

From the side of the mountain he saw the purple haze of twilight darken into the black of night. About eleven o'clock that night he was only part way up the mountain, nearly a hundred feet from the top. He kept on trying to climb, but he couldn't make it. Each step gained him little ground because he was too cold to climb. He had no coat or blanket, yet it was 22° below zero.

He became so sleepy that he no longer could keep his heavy eyelids open. He struggled to stay awake, for he knew that to sleep meant certain death. He hopped up and down and flung his arms back and forth, trying hard to stay awake and to keep warm.

At last he saw the first pink rays of the sunrise color the sky and he started to climb again. He was fairly close and tried to crawl the last few feet, but he just couldn't go any farther. Suddenly he became dizzy and felt the world swirling around him. He stopped and hung on tightly. Then once more his mind began to think clearly, just as it had when he had almost fallen from Mount Ritter. It seemed almost as if a voice was saying to him, "Don't try to go on. Return to safety."

Muir was disappointed to turn back, but he knew he must, so he returned to camp. After securing both rest and food, he made plans to try again. He studied a new map carefully and decided that this time he would try to climb the mountain from the east side. One of the

men in camp said, "Mount Whitney can't be climbed from the east side."

Muir just nodded and set off for his climb. Then, on October 21, he stood at the summit of Mount Whitney, the first man ever to have reached the top from the eastern side.

During the coming months he continued his mountain climbing. He never wore special clothes or shoes and usually carried only some dry bread and tea leaves for food. He hiked through the woods without fear of wild animals, and wild animals had no need to fear him. Sometimes he guided other people through the magnificent mountains and valleys, but much of the time he explored on his own for his personal pleasure.

That winter he went down from the mountains to Oakland to write a series of articles. He found it hard as an active mountain climber to sit still and write. He started out rapidly as if climbing rocky cliffs, with his thoughts coming faster than he could possibly write. When he started to describe one flower or one animal, he made the whole picture come into view. He just could not separate one part of nature from the whole of nature.

During the winter when he was writing, he saw his friends Professor and Mrs. Ezra Carr and met several other interesting people. Some of them visited him and listened to him read the articles which he was attempting to write. "Write everything just as you would say it," they suggested to him.

Previously Muir had written articles which were published in *Overland Magazine*. While he was in Oakland he met Dr. and Mrs. John Strentzel, who admired his articles. They invited him to visit them in their home in the Alhambra Valley, which he did much later.

After he had taken his articles "Studies in the

Sierra" to the magazine office, he walked on down the street. On the way he happened to see a wilted goldenrod growing by the pavement. At once he felt limp like the plant, and he knew he had to go back to the mountains. He ran back to his room and gathered up his belongings. Then he shouted happily, "I'm going wild once more!"

He hurried back to the mountains as rapidly as possible. Once more at night he lay on his back to watch the bright stars in the sky. By sunlight he climbed the jagged rocks, hung in the misting falls, and tramped through the mountain valleys.

In November he set out to climb Mount Shasta, with a guide to accompany him on the first part of the trip. When evening came they camped on the upper edge of the timberline. The next morning Muir started to climb the mountain alone and the guide went back to the bottom. Muir reached the top safely and spent several hours at the summit exploring volcanic rocks and the flowing glaciers of ice.

When he started back to camp the sky was dark with storm-filled clouds. He knew that a mountain storm was brewing that would be wild and beautiful. Looking at the heavy sky, he felt sure it would last for several days.

At once he started to prepare a safe place to enjoy the storm. He carved out a small cavelike hollow in a block of lava. He stacked up a wall of pine chunks and built a crackling, cozy fire. He wrapped himself in his warm blanket and snuggled down to enjoy an exciting event. By not eating too much, he had enough food to last for several weeks.

The fierce snowstorm blasted down the mountain. The air was thick with fine powdery snowflakes, tossed about by strong winds. The snow settled on Muir's blanket until it was over three inches thick. He watched the birds feeding on the pine cones and huddling close to tree trunks. He watched mountain sheep hovering under pine trees and even saw squirrels running and frolicking without fear across his blanket. He smiled as he watched them.

Warm and cozy, Muir felt nestled in the center of the storm. He watched the grand fury of the snow changing and softening the outlines of the mountains. In the distance he heard the crunch of horses' hooves on the snow. He sat up and listened more carefully.

Soon a shadowy form came near and Muir recognized the guide who had first helped him climb the mountain. "John! John Muir! Are you all right?" called the guide.

Muir sighed. He didn't want to be rescued, and at first he didn't answer. "Hey, I say!" the guide called again. "Are you all right?"

"Of course I'm all right," Muir finally replied. "But why have you come here? I could have come on down the mountain by myself."

"We've been worried about you," explained the guide. "I've brought an extra horse for you to ride down."

Muir wasn't ready to leave, but since the guide had gone to so much trouble, he broke camp. Reluctantly he rode down the mountainside out of the storm.

In December he visited friends on the divide between the Yuba and Feather River basins. The day after he got there, a bad storm came up. He borrowed a coat and went hiking in the woods to see the trees in the wind. He climbed to the top of a towering Douglas fir.

He clung to the tree as it swung back and forth in the heavy winds. With his strong arms holding to limbs and his legs clutching the trunk, he clung like a rider on a bucking bronco. He stayed there for hours listening to the pine needles singing in the wind. Time and again he heard the gusts of wind roar as they lashed about him in the treetop.

Day after day Muir hiked up and down the beautiful mountains. Everywhere he went he saw the results of man's damage to nature. He saw how the grass was destroyed where the sheep had overgrazed the meadows. He was shocked when he saw how the pines and fir trees about Lake Tahoe had been cut down and wasted.

Already much of the fine timberland was being claimed by private companies. Mountains and valleys were being combed by big mining companies in search of gold, silver, and other valuable minerals. Huge tracts of land and even streams and lakes were being purchased for business purposes.

Muir found many telltale signs of man taking over the wilderness. Here was a sign on a tree

130

claiming a valley for stock raising. Nearby was a sawmill chewing up giant sequoia trees. In the mountains there was a mining camp which warned visitors to keep out.

Muir now realized that he had to write articles to tell the people of the nation what was happening to the wilderness. Again he came down from the mountains to write. This time he went to the home of a prominent educator friend, John Swett, in San Francisco. For the next five years, whenever he came to the city to write, he stayed with this friend.

Swett was very much interested in Muir's efforts to save natural resources and gave him all the help he could. He often discussed conservation with him and introduced him to many friends who were eager to support him in this important activity for saving nature.

Off to Alaska

IN THE FALL after Muir visited Mount Shasta, he came down from the mountains eager to tell people about the wilderness. That winter he wrote and gave talks about the exciting places he had visited. He also wanted to let everyone know how important it was to save these wonders of nature.

As he wrote, he could see the back porch of a neighbor's house across the way. On the railing of the porch he noticed a simple little flower garden. It included only a single row of plants, a geranium, a tulip, a small rose bush, all growing in old cans.

132

Muir watched the members of the family as they came in and out. There was the father, who arrived with his lunch bucket at the end of the day. He was stooped and climbed the back steps as if he were very tired. Several young boys bounded in and out with their school books in their arms. There was no mother, but a slim young daughter looked after the family.

Muir watched her as she stopped her work to tend to her flowers. He saw the joy in her face as she watered the little garden. Lovingly she picked gently at the fading blossoms or brown leaves. A smile crossed her face as she leaned over to smell them.

Watching this girl, Muir could readily understand how happy she felt. He knew that every person needs some contact with nature to be truly happy and contented.

Once more Muir remembered how years

before he had wanted to make a park of Fountain Lake and Fern Lake in Wisconsin. He had wanted to save them so that everyone could enjoy their beauty. He felt that scenic parts of the wilderness should be turned into parks for people of the future to enjoy.

At once Muir started laying the foundation for a national park system in America. He traveled here and there in the West, looking for special parts of the wilderness that he felt should be saved. In a very short time he visited Utah, Nevada, and the San Gabriel Mountains. He also visited the Santa Cruz Mountains and Mount Shasta.

Muir now wanted to visit Alaska, but before leaving he went to see Dr. and Mrs. John Strentzel and their charming daughter Louie in the Alhambra Valley. While there he and Louie became engaged, but decided to postpone their marriage until he returned from

Alaska. "I want you to see Alaska because it will help you to round out your study of mountains and glaciers," said Louie.

Muir's trip to Alaska was one of the greatest events of his life. He traveled by ship to the town of Stickeen and became a close friend of the ship's engineer. Along the way the engineer told him about the logging camps in Oregon, Washington, and British Columbia. Muir was shocked to hear how many of the forests were being destroyed.

After many days of traveling Muir joined a group of missionaries, including S. Hall Young, who planned to preach to the Indians. They sailed up the Stickeen River on a boat called the *Cassiar*. As they cruised through the wild, mountainous country they passed glacier after glacier. Muir stood on deck and feasted his eyes on all the beautiful scenery.

Finally the group reached an old trading

post at Glenora. The captain informed everybody that the ship would stop there until morning. About seven or eight miles to the northeast Muir saw a magnificent group of mountains. At once he wanted to climb the highest peak to see all the surrounding mountains and glaciers. "What time is it now?" he asked the captain.

"Twenty minutes past three," replied the captain, eyeing him curiously.

"Good!" exclaimed Muir. "I'll have time to climb that mountain peak before you leave."

"I'm afraid not," warned the captain. "Remember, it's midafternoon now."

"I think I can make it to that highest mountain before sunset," answered Muir.

Mr. Young was standing near and overheard Muir's statement. "I'd like to go along with you on the climb," he said.

"I don't think you ought to go," replied

Muir. "I will have to hike at least fourteen miles before I actually climb the mountain. It will be a very difficult trip."

"I'm a good hiker," answered Young," and I like to climb."

Muir smiled but shook his head. "We have only a half day to do what usually requires a full day for an experienced mountain climber," he said.

"I am a very strong hiker and climber," Young insisted. "I won't hold you back."

At once Muir and Young set out on foot for the mountain. Muir pushed on rapidly and Young proved to be a strong walker. They reached the glacier about a half hour before sunset. Muir crawled around a steep point up the mountain where the rock was crumbling. "Be careful!" he shouted. "Climbing here is very dangerous."

Young was only a few feet behind, but Muir

137

could not see him. Suddenly he heard Young scream for help. He scrambled back to find Young hanging over the edge of a drop which went down for a thousand or more feet. He was clutching desperately to little crumbling knobs of rock and his body hung limply from his outstretched arms.

Swiftly and skillfully Muir managed to get below Young's body. He touched one of Young's feet and said, "You can't slip past me. I am below and will help you."

Muir moved slightly to lean against a rock and to get a more secure foothold. Then he gently pulled Young over the top of the rock. Young's eyes were closed, but he cried out weakly, "My arms! My arms are dislocated!"

Muir was stunned. He knew that he had to get Young someplace to find out how badly he was hurt. He looked at the treacherous rocks and found scarcely any footholds in sight. Fi-

nally he managed to make a few footholds by scraping the rocks. Then he pulled and rolled Young to a ledge where he could try to help him. Young's white face twisted with pain and he bit his lips as Muir tried to pull his arms back into place.

Muir could see that Young was suffering terrible pain and finally gave up. He knew he couldn't set Young's arms on this narrow rock. He took off his tie and suspenders and tied them around Young's arms and body to help relieve the pain. Then he said, "Lie still. I'll be back in a few minutes."

Young opened his eyes and nodded weakly. "I'll try to be quiet," he said.

"You're on solid ground," explained Muir. "You don't have to worry about slipping."

Muir climbed down and chipped out a foothold. Then he slid Young down to where his heel fitted into the notch. Young leaned back against the wall. Muir climbed down another five or six feet and dug out another foothold. Then he slid Young down to this little shelf. Slowly and carefully he slid Young down the steep wall step by step. Finally about midnight they reached the glacier.

Again Muir tried to set Young's arms. He was able to get one arm into place, but he couldn't set the other one, so once more he bound it to Young's side. By now Young was exhausted and shaking with pain.

"Do you think you can walk from here on?" asked Muir.

"Yes," Young answered bravely. He was suffering too much to say more.

Muir held onto Young and helped him walk slowly down the smooth surface of the glacier. After many stops to rest they finally reached a little stream. Young stretched out to relax while Muir started to build a fire. He made a warm crackling fire of fir chips and prepared a bed of leaves beside it for Young.

Gratefully Young stretched out on the leaves and warmed his tired, injured body by the fire. "You stay here and rest while I go down the mountain for help," said Muir, turning to leave. "I don't think you feel strong enough to walk any farther."

"No, please don't leave me!" cried Young, starting to get up. "I can walk."

"Lie still," ordered Muir. "The rest of the way back to the trading post is very rough and difficult. I won't be gone long and will get some help to carry you back."

"I can make it," Young insisted. "Please don't leave me."

Finally Muir decided to let Young walk from one rest stop to another. While Young was resting, he scouted ahead to find another place to stop. Then he built a fire and hurried back to

142

get Young. Finally, after making numerous stops, they got back to the boat long after sunrise, exhausted but happy.

When they got back, they found the captain angry because they were holding up the boat trip. As soon as he saw Young was injured, however, he ran down to help. During the coming weeks Young recovered and was very grateful to Muir for saving his life.

In the fall Muir and Young set out by canoe with Indian guides to explore the north shore. Much of the time they steered through floating icebergs and cold driving rain. Muir climbed a ridge fifteen hundred feet high from where he could see five glaciers pouring their floods into the salt water of the sea. He was the first explorer to see the region which was later named Glacier Bay.

As winter approached, the Indian guides became anxious to get started southward toward their homes. They were afraid that they would be trapped with their canoes in some of the inlets by the winter's ice and snow. If they were caught in the frozen waters they wouldn't be able to get out until the following spring or summer.

At first Muir wanted to stay in Alaska a while longer. He recalled that he had found winter one of the most exciting times of the year to explore the wilderness. Now he was eager to see what the Alaskan wilderness was like in winter. At last, however, he agreed to turn back southward with the Indians.

Once he left Alaska, his thoughts turned to California. Now he was eager to reach there because he soon was to be married. His bride-to-be, Louie Strentzel, was still waiting for him with her parents in the Alhambra Valley.

Exploring Alaska
with a Dog

AFTER MUIR returned from Alaska in the spring of 1880, he and Louie Strentzel were married. They settled down in a little house on her father's ranch in the Alhambra Valley. There Muir started to work in the orchards and vineyards on the ranch.

Muir was very happy working on the fruit ranch, but he greatly missed exploring the wilderness. One early summer evening he and Louie sat in the yard talking. He told her how he missed traveling. "I understand," she said. "While you are waiting for the fruit to ripen, why not take another trip to Alaska?"

"Thank you, Louie," said Muir. "That's a good idea, and I'll make arrangements to go."

Shortly he boarded a steamer headed north to Alaska. When the ship reached Fort Wrangell, he was surprised to find his old friend, S. Hall Young, standing on the dock. He called to Young, who could scarcely believe his eyes.

Muir laughed at Young's surprise. He ran down the gangplank shouting, "When can you be ready to go exploring with me? Get your canoe and crew and let's be off."

Immediately Young made plans to join Muir. He hired an Indian with a trustworthy canoe and two other Indians as crew members. These Indians knew the wilderness well and could serve as guides.

At last the canoe was packed with all the supplies needed for the trip. Muir took his place and the crew was ready to start. Young stood on the dock and said good-bye to the

146

members of his family. When he climbed into the canoe his little black dog, Stickeen, faithfully hopped in with him.

Muir smiled as he watched the little dog curl up on a pile of supplies. "Hand him back to your family on the dock," he said to Young.

When Young tried to pick him up Stickeen just crawled further into the blanket. Young laughed and said, "I think he wants to go with us, and he won't be any trouble."

The Indians shoved the canoe off and glided northward through the water. As they paddled their way through channels and inlets, Stickeen spent most of the day sleeping. Whenever they landed, however, he leaped out of the canoe to run on shore and was the last to come aboard when they shoved off.

Swiftly the Indians guided the canoe through the shining waters to Sumdum Bay. Muir explored the eastern inlet and made a map of the area. He named the glacier at the head of the inlet Young Glacier after his friend.

Next the Indians crossed the main bay to travel up the western inlet. They paddled for twenty miles with huge icebergs rocking back and forth all around them. Just before dark they started to shout to let Muir knew that they had come to the main glacier, which he was seeking.

That night they camped on a narrow strip of land by the water. Muir felt calm and happy as he fell asleep. Stickeen curled up on the blanket beside him. There with his bright eyes he lay watching his newly chosen master.

Early the next morning, as the first rays of sunlight appeared in the sky, Muir set out to climb and explore. He wanted to climb high enough to see the glacier and the bays and inlets. Stickeen trotted along behind him.

Muir breathed hard from climbing when he

148

reached the top. He looked at his map, which had been made seventy years before, but couldn't find two rivers of ice which spread out before him. These rivers had been formed by the glacier since the map had been made.

Later the Indians paddled into Stephens Passage and the group camped on Douglas Island beside a creek bed. Muir explored the edge of the creek and suddenly stooped down to examine the gravel more closely. "What do you see, John?" asked Young.

Muir merely shook his head. He walked a little farther and knelt down again to sift some of the gravel through his hands. "I think," he said quietly, "I have found some quartz with traces of gold."

"Oh," cried Young with excitement, "do you really think so? You may have made a wonderful discovery."

Muir held up the gravel and let it drop

149

through his hands. This time he was sure that the gravel contained quartz. "Yes, I may have made a wonderful discovery," he said.

The next day as they were breaking camp they met two gold prospectors. Muir told them about discovering the quartz and they decided to camp here, too. A short time later they found rich quartz deposits nearby. The next summer two important companies started gold mining here. This led to a gold rush and the founding of the town of Juneau.

The Indians now took Muir and Young on to Cross Sound to look for unexplored inlets. Their canoe was tossed about wildly on the huge waves from the cape. They couldn't find a place to land safely at the edge of the bay. Only Stickeen slept peacefully. All the rest of the crew were excited and worried.

At last they reached an inlet which is now called Taylor Bay. All members were glad to

150

land safely. At once they set up a camp in a spruce grove near the front of a large glacier, ready to start exploring.

Muir and Young hurried to the glacier. They discovered that it had moved forward recently, uprooting many trees in its path. Both were amazed to see huge, old trees pushed down by the ice flow.

That night Muir was so anxious to climb the glacier that he could scarcely go to sleep. The next morning he awoke early and heard rain falling on his tent. At once he stuffed a bread-crust into his pocket to eat later and hurried to join the storm.

It was still dark when he crawled from his tent. He bent his head as he stepped into the wet, driving rain. The wind blew so fiercely that he could hardly walk, but he was delighted to be joining the storm. He felt that he had learned some of his finest lessons from storms, but in all his explorations he was always careful to travel with storms and not against them.

Everyone in camp was still asleep as Muir started out. After he had taken only a few steps, he felt something at his heels. He stopped quickly and the little shadow of Stickeen stopped, too. "Go back, Stickeen!" he shouted to him.

A blast of rain struck the little dog, but he didn't move. Muir shouted above the noise of the storm. "Go back, Stickeen! Why are you following me? You must be crazy. There's nothing but bad weather ahead."

Stickeen cowered a little but still didn't move. Instead he begged to go by staring with his shining brown eyes and by wagging his plumy tail just a little.

Muir set his jaw. "Stickeen," he ordered, "you cannot come. Do you understand?" He pointed to the tent and said sternly, "Go back to camp and keep warm, get a good breakfast, and be sensible. I can't carry you over the rough places to protect you. Besides, the severe storm is likely to kill you somewhere along the trail."

Stickeen dropped his head and held his tail limply between his legs. Slowly he started back to the tent. Muir straightened up and started to walk on, but soon discovered that Stickeen was again at his heels.

The little dog was soaked with rain but blinked his eyes bravely. By his repeated actions he seemed to be saying, "If you must go, so must I."

Muir shook his head. "The earth might as well try to get rid of the moon," he said. "Come on if you must."

He took his crust of bread from his pocket and gave it to Stickeen. Then he and the little

153

dog set off to climb the glacier. Little did he realize it, but this was to become one of the most exciting days of his life.

At once he and Stickeen started to climb the glacier in the raging storm. Along the way he found a shelter where they could crawl in out of the rain. From here he could see the tree-covered mountain on one side and the ice crags of the glacier on the other. Also he could hear the exciting noises of the storm, including the different tones of branches of trees, loose rocks, and pieces of ice being blown past by the wind. Stickeen was frightened and snuggled close beside him for safety.

After the storm died down, Muir and Stickeen climbed out over the glacier. He felt a warmth of friendship for the dog as they traveled along together. Soon he discovered when he looked down that the dog's feet had been cut by sharp ice and were leaving a trail of

154

blood. Quickly he took out his handkerchief and tore it apart to make moccasins or slippers for the dog's sore paws.

The glacier seemed fairly safe, so he decided to cross to the other side. He walked carefully and used his compass to guide him. When he came to cracks in the ice, he jumped over them and Stickeen leaped over behind him. Much of the time they traveled in partial darkness, but there was an occasional burst of sunlight. In the sunlight Muir could see the gleaming glacier from side to side.

When they reached the west side of the glacier, Muir walked north as far as possible into the Fairweather Mountains. Suddenly he came to a branch of the glacier, which looked like a frozen, rushing mountain stream. He stood and watched a magnificent cascade pour blocks of ice into a lake, filling it with icebergs.

Muir decided to turn back, with Stickeen

following him, but soon they were overtaken by a blinding snowstorm. After traveling about two miles across the glacier they came to a network of cracks in the ice. Muir traced the cracks carefully as he made his way forward. Stickeen leaped each crevasse bravely in order to stay close at Muir's heels.

Muir tried to go as fast as he could while it was still daylight, but dusk fell fast and the crevasses became deeper and wider. He followed them up and down like a maze to find places to jump across. Stickeen crouched and carefully leaped across after him.

Darkness hampered them and snow swirled about them. They found the going very slow. Muir wondered whether they would have to spend the night on this wilderness of ice.

After jumping a very wide crevasse, Muir hoped that he would find only smooth, unbroken ice ahead of them. At first all went well,

156

but soon he came to an even larger chasm which had to be crossed. Quickly he looked all about him and discovered that he and Stickeen were on an island of ice. They were surrounded and trapped by an enormous canyon about forty or fifty feet wide.

Muir looked all about for a way to escape. As always before, in a moment of sheer disaster, he was able to think clearly. Far below he could see a slender bridge of ice across the deep canyon. It hung from one side to the other like a loose rope, with its ends fastened to the sides eight to ten feet below the top.

Muir looked down the steep straight wall of ice and up the other side and pressed his lips together tightly. Never had he been faced with a more dangerous situation. Stickeen came to look, too. He perked up his pointed ears and stared down at the deep valley of ice and the thin rope of ice across it. Then he looked up at

Muir and started to whine and cry. Like his master, he wondered what they could do.

Calmly Muir leaned over and started to carve steps in the cold hard wall of ice. Carefully carving steps ahead of him, he slowly lowered himself from foothold to foothold. Up above he could hear Stickeen crying, but he did not dare look up at him.

He steadied himself against the wind and lowered himself in constant danger. Slowly he kept going until he reached the narrow bridge of ice. Finally with great difficulty he managed to balance himself astride the rope of ice.

Slowly he crawled and hitched his way across the narrow bridge of ice. As he crawled, he carved out a path four inches wide for Stickeen to use. Although he had left the dog behind, he was still hoping that Stickeen would follow him.

When he reached the opposite wall, with

almost superhuman strength he hacked and carved footholds to reach the top. At once he turned to look across the chasm at Stickeen. In the distance he could see the dog trembling with fear and clinging to the edge of the island with his small booted feet. "Come on, Stickeen," he called with outstretched arms. "Come on, wee doggie. I'm sure you can make it."

Stickeen stood quietly and listened, but when he looked down he started to howl. He paced back and forth, crying loudly. Across the chasm Muir walked off as if he were leaving. After taking a few steps he paused and called, "I guess I'll have to go on without you if you don't come."

Stickeen cowered and shook. Surrounded by darkness and fear, he slowly started down the wall of ice. With cautious footsteps he safely made it down to the bridge of ice. Again he looked down into the icy depths below. Then, shivering, he looked up pitifully at his master. Muir now felt encouraged and once more held out his arms to the dog. "Come on, wee doggie," he called. "You're on your way."

Slowly Stickeen edged his way across the bridge of ice in the path Muir had cut for him. When he reached the end, he stopped to look up at the sheer cliff of ice. Suddenly with a burst of courage he scrambled up the wall and over the brink to the top.

Once he was safe, he jumped and barked with joy. He ran around in circles, leaping up on Muir with his tongue hanging out and his big brown eyes glistening brightly. He was only a dog, but he was happy to have proved that he was a good traveler, too.

Briefly Muir sank down on the ice in relief while Stickeen bounded about him. Then he took off for camp with the dog following close behind. They struggled into camp long after

Young and the Indian guides had given up hope of their return that night.

They were both so exhausted they couldn't eat. Stickeen crawled off to his blanket in the tent. Muir sank down before the fire to dry his frozen clothes and Young brought him some hot coffee to drink. Until now Muir hadn't said a word. At last, after drinking three cups of coffee, he pointed to Stickeen and said weakly, "Yon's a brave doggie."

"He must be," agreed Young. "I don't see how he managed to keep up with you on such a dangerous trip."

"Neither do I," said Muir, still speaking weakly, "but he has been one of the most exciting traveling companions I have ever had. Someday I may even want to write a book to tell people about him."

162

Joining
a Rescue Party

AFTER MUIR returned from his second trip to Alaska, he worked hard on the ranch through the fall and winter and felt happy and contented. Occasionally he thought about some of his explorations in Alaska and especially about Stickeen. When spring came he and Louie had their first child, a daughter, whom they named Annie Wanda. They were delighted with this new member of the family.

When Muir was in the middle of his spring work he was invited to make another trip north. On this trip he would travel on the ship *Corwin* to search for the crew of the ship *Jean-*

nette, which had been lost in Arctic waters. At first he refused and said that he could not possibly go at this time.

Louie felt that Muir should join the searching party. "John," she said, "I think it would be good for you to get away. There is no need for you to stay home. I am very well and Annie Wanda is a healthy, happy baby."

Muir accepted and in early May sailed north with the search party. The *Corwin* steamed through storm-tossed waters. When it came into Unalaska Bay in the Aleutian Islands huge waves rolled in and crashed against its bow.

Muir spent much time in the pilot house, where the captain guided the ship. He was filled with excitement as he looked at the stern cliffs and ice-covered mountains looming against the gray sky. For the first time in his life, his thoughts were divided. Although he reveled in the beautiful, wild landscape

164

around him, he kept wishing that he were back in sunny Alhambra Valley with Louie and the baby.

A month later, the *Corwin* slowly made its way through the waters off the coast of Siberia. The crew of the *Jeannette,* which had set out in 1879 on a polar expedition, had disappeared in this area. The search party of the *Corwin* followed every possible clue to hunt for the lost men aboard the missing vessel.

When the ship reached East Cape, Muir climbed up three thousand feet and looked down on the cold waters of Bering Strait. From this high point he hoped to catch a glimpse of the thirty-three men who had been lost. Little did he know that they were still wandering about, struggling to stay alive in the wild, snowy wasteland to the northwest.

Only three weeks before the *Jeannette* had pulled free from the ice off Herald Island. The ship had been so badly damaged that it had begun to sink. Before it sank, however, the captain and crew had escaped with their supplies, including dogs, sleds, and small boats. Then they had started on a five-hundred-mile journey over the ice and open water, hoping to reach Siberia.

Muir and the search party could find no trace of the lost *Jeannette's* crew, so they headed for Herald Island. When they came near they moored the *Corwin* on an ice floe a short distance away. Hurriedly some of the landing party started out over huge blocks of ice, hoping to reach the island.

Muir stood and watched as these members left. Then, using a spyglass, he looked toward the island carefully and mapped another route for himself. Immediately he set off with two or three men by a longer but easier route and managed to reach the island. The others, strug-

166

gling up a cliff, were turned back by falling rocks. They went back to the ship saying that it was impossible to reach Herald Island.

Muir walked back and forth across the island, looking for signs of the lost crew but could find nothing. Before he left he climbed to the summit of the island and saw the cliffs of Wrangel Island forty miles away.

He wanted to spend the night on the island in the clear Arctic twilight. Before long, however, he heard the captain's voice calling, "Come quickly! We have to hurry. There are ten miles of dangerous ice-filled waters between us and the open sea."

Slowly the *Corwin* worked its way toward Wrangel Island. Gradually, with a full head of steam, the ship pushed and forced its way through the ice to shore. Then the captain took possession of Wrangel Island in the name of the United States. This was the first time any explorers had set foot on this island, which today is part of the Soviet Union.

The members of the search party looked for traces of the *Jeannette's* crew but found nothing. They started to explore the island but soon were called back to the ship. They had to leave because the ice was closing in rapidly. Before they left, however, the captain and Muir planted an American flag on the island.

The *Corwin* escaped from the ice pack with great difficulty and headed home. At that time the thirty-three starving men from the *Jeannette* were still trying to cross the frozen wasteland of the islands of New Siberia. They struggled to reach the Siberian coast in their three small boats, but only a few survived.

When the *Corwin* first stopped for mail on the way home, Muir stood at the rail to take the letters. He handed them out to the rest of the men, but could hardly wait to find one for him-

self. There at the bottom of the stack he found a letter from Louie. Quickly he read the letter and gave a sigh of relief to learn that she and the baby were fine.

At Unalaska the *Corwin* stopped for mail again. Here Muir received more letters with cheerful news from home. He felt very fortunate to have such a devoted and understanding wife waiting for him.

After his return from Alaska Muir settled down on the ranch with his family. He spent his time managing the business of the ranch and became very successful in raising Tokay grapes and Bartlett pears. One of his closest neighbors was his old friend John Swett, who had bought a ranch nearby.

In January, 1886, Muir and his wife had a second little girl, Helen, born to them. She was a very frail little baby who required constant attention. For this reason Muir stayed close to the ranch for a number of months in case he was needed to help care for her.

During this time, even though Muir was working on the ranch, he could not forget about the wilderness. He thought of how important it was to save forests in the mountains. It made him angry to know that many trees were being cut down and the grasslands destroyed. If these destructive things continued he felt certain that the whole of nature would be ruined.

Muir felt deeply that people needed to be able to wander in the wilderness to renew their spirits. He often thought about the family with the little back porch garden which he had seen years before. He knew that everyone needs to return to nature from time to time to be refreshed.

At this time Muir helped to write two legislative bills to be introduced in Congress. One was to make larger grants for the Yosemite and Mariposa Big Tree Grove. The other was to set apart a tract of land in California, including Kings Canyon and the Sequoia grove, as a public park. Neither of these bills passed.

In the spring of 1887 Muir was asked to help prepare two large books of nature studies to be called *Picturesque California*. His wife encouraged him to work on these books. He accepted and settled down to write along with managing the ranch at the same time.

Helping Found
a National Park

WEARILY MUIR managed the ranch and tried to write *Picturesque California*. After each day's work he sat at his desk trying to put his thoughts into words. He wrote page after page and then stopped to read what he had written. Somehow, however, he just couldn't seem to put the right words on paper to describe the beauty and wonder of the mountains of California.

Louie worried about him and knew that he wasn't satisfied with his writing. She noted that he walked with a slow step and that he had a bad cough. She realized that he had to get back to nature for a while to restore his usual abundant energy and enthusiasm.

One of Muir's friends invited him to go to Lake Tahoe to help study flowering plants. Louie was delighted and Muir accepted the invitation to make the trip. Once more he was happy to get back to the mountains.

Soon he and William Keith, the artist who was drawing illustrations for *Picturesque California*, took a trip to Mount Shasta. This was the first mountain trip he and Keith had taken together in ten years.

When they reached Mount Shasta, Muir was shocked by the destruction that had taken place in the surrounding forests. He felt sad to find that many of the beautiful trees which he had seen here before were gone. "Maybe we can still do something to protect the forests," he said to Keith. "In our book we can include a chapter to recommend that Shasta be made into a national park to save its beauty for lovers of nature to enjoy."

From Mount Shasta Muir and Keith went on to Seattle, Washington, to climb Mount Rainier. There they were joined by six other men who also wanted to climb the mountain. On their way up they camped next to a clear mountain lake where Keith started to draw some of the nearby scenery.

Muir smiled as he looked upward at the great snow-covered mountain peak. He could hardly wait to start climbing again. Early the next morning he and six other men set out to work their way up the mountain. They half crawled up slopes of gravel, struggled up icy cliffs, and crossed canyons of ice.

They climbed for seven and one-half hours and finally reached the top. Muir now sat apart from the others to enjoy the beautiful view of the endless forests and mountain peaks and valleys. At once, as if by miracle, he felt well and strong and full of energy again.

After Muir returned from his trip to Mount Shasta and Mount Rainier, he settled down to writing with enthusiasm. His mind was clear and fresh, and he could think of many exciting things to say. His words came freely and always proved to be the right ones.

In June, 1889, Robert Underwood Johnson, editor of *Century Magazine*, came to San Francisco to get some articles on California. While there he and Muir arranged to go camping together in Yosemite. Everywhere they went they saw signs of destruction. There were burnt stumps of trees. The undergrowth was trampled and chewed by sheep. Even the streams and waterfalls were being polluted.

Muir was grief-stricken by the damage. He and Johnson sat around the campfire and talked about the destruction which was taking

176

place. Finally Johnson said, "Let us work together to make this Yosemite into a national park so that it can be saved for the future."

Muir shook his head. He recalled that in 1864 Abraham Lincoln had turned Yosemite Valley over to California for a state park. "Already this valley is a state park, but see how people are destroying it," he said.

"You're right," replied Johnson. "Prepare articles for me to publish, urging that Yosemite be converted into a national park to preserve its beauty."

At first Muir was fearful that Johnson's plan wouldn't work. He told him about the two bills which he had helped prepare to establish national parks in the area, but that both had been defeated by Congress.

Johnson was still hopeful. "Go ahead and prepare articles telling the wonders of Yosemite. Outline the boundaries for the park and

177

explain the need to save the wilderness. In the meantime I'll have some of my political friends introduce a bill in Congress."

Muir was enthusiastic and started to write. Besides writing magazine articles, he also wrote many news stories. Johnson returned east and began to make plans to have a bill on Yosemite introduced in Congress.

After Muir had finished his writing, he decided to take another trip to Alaska. He wanted to visit Muir Glacier, which had been named after him. His doctor said, "John, you won't be able to make this trip. You are not well enough."

Muir laughed as he answered, "You're wrong. The trip will do me good."

When he arrived in Alaska, he planned a sled trip across the glacier. He put heavy new soles on his shoes to get good footholds on the ice. He made a sleeping bag out of bearskin and

red wool to keep himself warm when he settled down for the night.

Early in the evening he camped on the glacier. He shaved a few splinters from the bottom part of his sled and started a fire in one of his tin cups. Then he made his tea in the other cup over the flame. After he drank his tea, he snuggled down in the sleeping bag on the sled and slept cozily and comfortably through the night.

The next morning when he crossed the glacier, he felt fit and healthy again. He no longer had a cough. As always, he had picked up strength while living with nature.

When Muir returned to California the Yosemite campaign was at its peak. Largely because of his writings and Robert Johnson's work, a park bill had been introduced in Congress. All nature lovers supported the bill, but a few selfish-minded people fought it strongly.

Fortunately, the Secretary of the Interior, inspired by Muir's articles, worked hard for the bill. On October 1, 1890, the bill was passed by Congress and Yosemite Park was established. At once the government sent a cavalry troop to patrol the area. As a result of the growing enthusiasm to save forests, Sequoia and General Grant National Parks were created in the same year.

Today Yosemite Park is one of the most scenic and popular national parks in America. It is located about 200 miles east of San Francisco and includes about 1200 square miles of natural wonderland. Chiefly it consists of a huge canyon bordered by the Sierra Nevada with numerous picturesque waterfalls tumbling from the mountains.

The park abounds with trails which lead to deep forests, sparkling lakes, rushing streams, and jagged peaks. It contains numerous kinds of trees, including groves of the famous Sequoia Gigantea, or Big Trees. Besides trees, hundreds of other kinds of plants may be found on the grounds.

Many kinds of animals roam about the park, including bears and deer. In addition, over 200 species of birds fly about the valley and mountains. All these forms of wild life continue to live here just as they have for hundreds of years in the past.

Busy Final Years

WITH EACH passing year John Muir realized more and more the need for preserving the wilderness. He felt that the beauty of nature should be saved so that both men and women and boys and girls could enjoy the wonders of the great outdoors.

He realized that it was necessary to preserve both trees and mountains so that all of nature could be saved. He knew that all of nature works together. It was impossible to cut down the trees on the mountains and still have beautiful valleys with rivers and waterfalls. It was impossible to allow sheep to destroy all the green grasses without having dirt sliding down into the valleys. If all plants were destroyed, even the water supply itself would be destroyed, too.

In 1892, John Muir and a group of men who were vitally interested in saving the wilderness founded the Sierra Club. Muir was elected its first president. The purpose of this newly-founded club was to work for the conservation of nature.

The club was founded just in time, because a bill was presented in Congress to take away nearly half of the Yosemite National Park. Lumbermen wanted to cut down the trees and stockmen wanted to use the parkland for grazing their sheep.

John Muir and the Sierra Club fought hard to save Yosemite National Park. Finally, after a long struggle, they succeeded, and all nature lovers were thankful. If it had not been for their efforts, Yosemite National Park might not exist for people's enjoyment today.

As a member of the Sierra Club Muir wrote many articles in which he sought to share the beauty and excitement of the mountains with the American people. He tried to encourage everyone to work to save the wilderness. Robert Johnson published many of his articles in *Century Magazine* and talked with many important men in government. Other members of the Sierra Club worked hard to get the government to preserve natural resources.

As a result of the Sierra Club's efforts, President Benjamin Harrison set aside more than 13,000,000 acres of watershed land in the United States as forest reserves. The most important of these areas in California was the Sierra Forest Reserve. Unfortunately, however, this reserve was not adequately patrolled. Lumbermen kept right on cutting down trees in the forest, and stockmen kept on grazing sheep in the meadows. They simply paid no attention to the law.

John Muir now took time off to revisit his old home in Scotland. He also visited England and several other countries in Europe. He especially enjoyed visiting Switzerland, where he was fascinated by the mountains.

In 1894 Muir wrote a book entitled *The Mountains of California*. In this book he urged people to take action to protect our natural resources. The book was widely read and led to many important reforms.

About this time, Muir was asked to join a special group to study the problems of saving forests and water supplies. He and the other members traveled through several western states. They visited the great forests of Washington and Oregon, Crater Lake of California, and Grand Canyon of Arizona. Everywhere they went they saw destruction from mining, lumbering, and sheep raising. They even found mines in the Grand Canyon.

In the 1890's President Grover Cleveland took strong steps to preserve forest lands. He celebrated the 165th birthday of George Washington by setting aside thirteen reservations to protect forests. In addition he approved the establishment of Grand Canyon and Mount Rainier as national parks.

The men in the lumber business, mining business, and sheep raising business objected furiously. At once they set about to try to stop Cleveland's act of establishing these areas of national forests. They even threatened to try to impeach him.

For a time these selfish businessmen succeeded in preventing Cleveland from setting aside the forest preserves and at first the outlook seemed hopeless. Muir was very angry and upset to find that these selfish men could hold up such a worthy project. He put aside all his other work to help carry on this important fight.

He wrote a strong article, "American Forests," which appeared in the *Atlantic Monthly Magazine.* In this article he explained that trees are helpless to protect themselves from selfish men in search of dollars. He concluded his article by saying, "Through all the wonderful, eventful centuries God has cared for these trees; but he cannot save them from fools—only Uncle Sam can do that."

In the spring of 1899 Muir was invited to join a group of noted scientists on an expedition to Alaska. This group was interested in finding out how important Alaska could become in the future. Muir led a group over the moraine at Glacier Bay to help them study the natural surroundings. He made many friends who

188

later helped him in his fight to help save the trees and the mountains.

While Theodore Roosevelt was President he made a special trip to California to go camping with John Muir. The first night they camped alone under the giant sequoias in Yosemite Park. The next day they rode horseback to Glacier Point. At sunset they camped in a meadow in the highlands. Muir built a roaring campfire and the two cooked steaks over the flames. As the fire simmered down to a rosy glow, they stretched out on beds of fir and ferns. While they relaxed they talked about the need for saving the wilderness.

After the moon was high in the dark sky they finally rolled themselves in their blankets and fell asleep. In the morning when they awakened they were covered with snow. "This is bully!" shouted the President. "I wouldn't have missed this for anything!"

The last night they camped on the meadow beneath El Capitan. Again they talked of the need for saving the mountains and beautiful trees. "I'll certainly do all I can to save them," said President Roosevelt before he returned to Washington.

John Muir continued to delight in the glory of nature to the end of his days. He kept on traveling, writing, and lecturing on the need for preservation of the beautiful wilderness. He died in 1914, but his fame still lives on because of his many important contributions. During his life he wrote newspaper sketches, magazine articles, and books to describe his exciting adventures. Some of his best-known books are *A Thousand Mile Walk to the Gulf, My Travels in Alaska, The Mountains of California, Yosemite, Our National Parks,* and *Stickeen.* All of these books are still widely read and enjoyed today.

John Muir has been honored with many memorials, including John Muir Park at his boyhood farm in Wisconsin, Muir Trail in Sequoia National Park, Muir Glacier in Alaska, and Muir Woods at the end of the Golden Gate Bridge in California.

The most important memorial of all, however, is the National Park System which he strove so hard to strengthen and expand, especially Yosemite National Park in California.

Printed in the United States
By Bookmasters